Table of Contents

Claiming His Pack

Northbay Pack

Jena Wade
&
Lorelei M. Hart

Published in the United States of America

www.thejenawade.com

Warning

This book contains sexually explicit scenes and adult language and may be considered offensive to some readers. Jena Wade's books are for sale to adults ONLY, as defined by the laws of the country in which you made your purchase. Please store your files wisely, where they cannot be accessed by under-aged readers.

Chapter One

Dylan

I settled into the highback executive office chair that sat behind the enormous mahogany desk that had been hand-crafted by my omega grandfather, the long passed Alpha Omega of the Northbay pack. He'd built it as a gift for my grandfather after he was named Alpha of the pack nearly sixty years ago. My brother Ozzy had inherited our omega grandfather's gift for woodworking, while I'd inherited our alpha grandfather's gift for leadership—at least in theory.

My fingers traced the carving my grandfather did in the mahogany. I loved how much history there was to this desk, but I loathed the pressure that came with it. I had large paws to fill to be the Alpha that Northbay deserved, and some days I wasn't sure that I was the right wolf for the job.

Until I knew for sure, I had a job to do. I was most of the way through a budget document for the pack's finances when a knock sounded at the door. I paused and sniffed the air. The scent outside wasn't overly familiar. The person outside didn't feel like pack, not yet, but they were nonetheless.

"Come in," I called.

Darren, the newest member of my pack, walked in the door. His gaze was downcast as he sauntered across the room. He snuck a glance at the bookshelves that lined the walls. They were built into the wall and filled to the brim with literature from all genres. My omega father's passion was reading, and this room served as a secondary library for pack members as well as my office.

"Please sit," I said.

He bared his neck in submission, then sat down across from me.

Most of my pack members were born into the pack, or mated in after they met their mates, fated or not, within the pack. A few of my pack members had moved to other packs after finding their mates among them, my brother included. I missed having him around, but was happy he'd found such bliss.

In Darren's case, he had requested to join our pack after an unfortunate event surrounding his brother, and coincidentally my own brother as well, had occurred with his birth pack, Greycoast. His brother, in a misguided attempt to win the love of a mated alpha, had been an apprentice to a dark healer. Mitch had gone so far as to kidnap the omega, my brother Ozzy, to do him harm. Darren and Ozzy's alpha, Kade, had arrived in time to stop them from harming Ozzy, but not in time to stop Mitch from meeting his demise. The whole ordeal had been hard on the Greycoast pack, and it was understandable that Darren didn't wish to be reminded of his brother at every turn.

"You asked to see me, alpha?" he said.

"Yes, I wanted to see how you were settling in."

The dark circles under his eyes and the bloodshot whites of his eyes told me that he wasn't sleeping well, and whatever rest he got wasn't restful at all. He had lost at least ten pounds since moving here a few weeks ago. There was no spark to his eyes, and even his wolf was subdued and sullen.

"I'm doing all right," he said. "Just getting to know everybody."

"Great," I said. "I'm glad." Though I knew I would have to do more to keep an eye on him and bring him back to a more healthy state, I didn't wish to broach the subject just then. Darren had endured great tragedy and when he was ready, we'd address it, but for now he needed time to heal and process.

I folded my arms in front of me and leaned over the desk, giving Darren my full attention.

"I'd really like it if you would join my Betas," I said, not bothering to beat around the bush. I got straight to the point. I knew Darren appreciated the efficiency.

"For a meeting?" he said. "Sure, alpha, whatever you need."

"No. Permanently," I said. "I want you to *be* one of my Betas, in an official capacity."

Darren's eyebrows shot up, and he met my gaze fully for the first time. His wolf perked up, but then slunk back down. Darren shook his head. "I'm not qualified, sir, alpha. I'm too new."

Except he was qualified. He had to make some of the hardest decisions a pack leader ever had to make when it came to things with his brother. The way his former pack spoke of him with such pride… he was qualified in every way.

And I'd seen the brief interest in his eyes and his wolf. This was a role Darren was made for. I was surprised his previous alpha, Byrom, had never recruited him officially for the role. This wasn't going to be a hard sell. His wolf wasn't going to let him pass this up.

"As you may know, my father and grandfather were the two previous alphas. And they're both still alive, still members of the pack. It's an oddity not usually experienced amongst packs and because of it, we have a divide among us." It wasn't spoken, but it was there… always there. I could technically ask my father and grandfather to leave, to find a new pack to retire to, and they would. But it didn't feel right.

"The divide wasn't purposeful." I didn't want him to think less of my family. Not that he would. Darren had a good head on his shoulders. "And my family does what they can to curb the alliances some wolves have to their former alphas. But nonetheless, it remains. And it has made the pack feel weak and disjointed."

My grandfather had stepped down as alpha when his Alpha Omega had passed. Losing one's fated mate wasn't something a wolf handled well, but my grandfather was an oddity. My father had stepped down simply because he didn't enjoy the Alpha role. He'd been a good alpha for the pack, but he didn't prefer the limelight. My parents tended to stay in their own corner of pack lands. It was weird to have them here, but also not.

"I haven't—"

I cut off Darren's denial. "It's an unmistakable feeling that all of our wolves sense. It makes us restless. It doesn't help that I am without an Alpha Omega."

Darren nodded.

The legend was that when the alpha of the pack

found their fated mate, the rest of the pack would follow. But until then, there weren't many mates within the pack. It had definitely been the case for us.

In Greycoast, when Byrom had found his mate, several of his Betas had followed suit. And then other members of the pack. Here we'd had no such luck. Even now we had very few omegas that were of age. Our dorms that we specifically used to house omegas sat empty, and the few omegas we had that were unmated were barely of age and still lived at home with their parents.

"I don't know how I can help," Darren said. "I'm still an outsider."

"That is exactly what we need. Or at least, it may help. I'd like your input on things we can do better, things we can improve on. And things you might see that I do not." I didn't want to steal ideas from the Greycoast pack and even if I did, Byrom would be happy to share. No, I wanted the unique perspective only a newcomer could give. He didn't see things as *just the way things have always been,* and that was going to be huge. Or at least I hoped it would be.

"Do you think there will be an attempt to overthrow you?" His heart was beating in his chest and I wanted to kick myself for not being more clear. He'd seen what damage disloyal wolves could bring upon a pack first hand, and this situation wasn't that at all.

I shook my head. "Not from within. There might be wolves of mine that are unhappy, but not enough of them to start a rebellion of any kind. They're just restless." A stagnant pack will do that to a wolf. "Their loyalties have been to several different alphas, and it can confuse the wolf inside of us. But to the outside world, we may appear fragile and divided. I don't want any outside influence to think we might have a weakness."

"That makes sense." He rubbed his chin. "I'd be happy to help. If you think the Beta role is what is necessary for me, I'll do my best."

"Perfect. I'll assemble my Betas and we can have a meeting tomorrow mid-day." They would be relieved to have the help and I'd already felt them out. They liked Darren a lot. Even if he didn't fully feel their acceptance yet, it was there. "How about dinner at the pavilion? You know where we usually convene for Beta meetings, yes?"

"Yes, alpha, I do."

"Great, thank you, Darren."

Darren stood, baring his neck before turning around and leaving. For a split second it looked like he might have a question for me, but he just walked out. He had a lot to think about and there would be questions a plenty. I didn’t want to push him anymore than I already had by asking him what he’d been thinking. There was a fine line between pushing enough and pushing too much.

I returned my attention to the budget, but my heart wasn't in it. I needed to turn this particular task over to another pack member. But the budget was another one of our weaknesses. Though we were wolves, we lived in a human world and money was a thing that we needed to keep us protected from the outside world. Plus, there was no reason for us to live completely in the dark ages. We were also partially human, and as such we enjoyed some of the more human luxuries which also required money. We had phones, internet, and other technologies that we enjoyed. Our budget was tighter than I wanted it to be; our means of revenue for the pack were drying up and if we didn’t find new investments or business opportunities soon, we would be in trouble.

I sat back, ran a hand through my hair, and let out a long sigh. I couldn't help but think that several of these issues would be lessened if only I had an Alpha Omega at my side. Even if they didn't bring the calm to the pack that they supposedly did, it would be someone to keep me grounded. Someone I could confide in and cuddle with, share my worries and lean on for support. I longed for a mate like my grandfather had had before his omega had passed. My parents were another example of a mating that

I'd envied. They loved each other with all they had.

Maybe I was just lonely. I had a pack full of wolves surrounding me, but at the end of the day it was just me crawling into bed. And even the friends I had… I could never open up to them fully—not when I was Alpha. Some of my frustrations and worries needed to be mine alone—or mine and my Alpha Omega's. Why didn't this job come with an instruction manual?

I itched to simply call my father or grandfather to seek their advice, but I knew I couldn't always rely on them when the situation seemed dire. I needed to rely on my instincts as an alpha and as a wolf.

Perhaps a mating of convenience was in my future. The likelihood of my fated mate falling into my lap were slim to none. And the pack needed another leader to look up to. It wasn't as if there hadn't been offers, as old-fashioned as that was, but there were some packs who still used them almost exclusively, and a single Alpha was pretty tempting from that perspective.

I didn't love the idea of mating simply for the sake of mating, but the time could come where I didn't have a choice. I needed an Alpha Omega at my side, and my fated mate, though I wanted one desperately, wasn't likely to be in my future.

My wolf whined at the restlessness of my thoughts. It made my skin itch with the need to run and forget my worries for a moment, but instead I lifted my pen and went back to work on the budget. These numbers weren't going to balance themselves.

Chapter Two

Niko

One child.

Six omegas.

Twenty days.

Nineteen nights.

Thirteen hours.

Who knew how many minutes.

And still… I didn't feel like it was safe enough for us to stop. Not for longer than a drink, a kill, or a short nap. Shadowpine wasn't going to let us go. Not easily. And while we might've been ahead of them, we didn't have the luxury of letting our guard down.

Lives were at stake—ours.

I kept weaving through the trees, my paws crunching the leaves with each step. If it was just me, I'd have long given up. But it wasn't just me. They were counting on me—my brother was counting on me—my niece or nephew was counting on me—the omegas were counting on me—Kenon was counting on me. Giving up was not an option and so I carried on.

How strong and brave they all were, putting their trust in me, an omega, to keep them safe. Life was horrible in the Shadowpine pack—worse than most people could have ever imagined—but it was what we knew. What we were now facing could be a thousand times worse.

And yet they followed me.

I tilted my head up and scented deeply. Crap.

We'd been slowing all day, our bodies too exhausted, our adrenaline long gone. We were going to need to rest soon, but not yet—not with what I'd just scented.

I stopped, taking my skin as a signal to the others to do the same.

Piers, Lewis, and Ralf shifted. Ralf helped Kenon from his harness and Lewis took it off of Seymour, allowing him to shift. Cujo kept his fur. He always did. I wasn't even sure he could shift.

I was tired—bone tired, and Seymour was doing this with a child on his back. We'd offered to take turns, but he was protective. So protective. His little boy held his arms out for his father and Seymour held him close.

Thankfully Kenon was still able to feed from his father's breast. Something that had been a necessity for him to stay alive even at his age in Shadowpine was now the thing that allowed him a chance at freedom. Had he needed human food… I shivered at the choices we'd have had to make and would continue to have to make.

We'd been as far from society as we could be the entire time since our escape. We had to be. A pack of wolves would have farmers going for their guns. A pack of wolves with a child…that would not end well. And even if we came to a town, what were we going to do? It wasn't like we could walk right into a store and buy food. Clerks tended to not want naked people at their counter, especially naked people without money.

The little boy suckled as I attempted to form the words that were going to inevitably instill fear in them. We had two choices and neither of them was ideal.

"Piers, how are you holding up?" My brother was leaning against a tree, his arms cradling his belly. He was about halfway through his pregnancy and this exertion couldn't be good for either of them.

It's better than the alternative, I reminded myself.

"I could use a nosh." He winked. My brother was

such a trooper, an eternal optimist, and I appreciated his desire to comfort me, but I really needed to know.

"Piers," I said, a bit firmer.

"I hurt all over, I could eat a doe by myself, and I want to sleep for a week after a long, hot bath. Is that what you want to hear?" He plopped to the ground.

"No. That's not what I want to hear, but it's what I need to hear." I scented the air again. Yeah, it was decision time.

"Cujo, if you want a say, maybe shift?" I don't know why I bothered. If he was going to shift, he would have by now.

Everyone dealt with the horror of being sold with the sole purpose of breeding babies and working until you couldn't work anymore differently. My brother tried humor. The twins stuck together. Seymour focused on keeping his young safe. I got some sort of notion I could fix things. And Cujo—he wolfed out and stayed that way.

Heck, we didn't even know his name. Cujo was just an honorary nickname we gave him for being badass enough to bite his "mate" when the bastard bought him.

Sure, mating marks are the things dreams are made of to most mated pairs, but Cujo wasn't marking.

He was attempting to bite the alpha's dick off. The only reason I was glad he didn't was because they'd have put him down and then beat all the witnesses to show their power. Instead, his sadistic owner opted to try and *break* him, and for all I knew he had, just not in the way he'd intended.

I still hated that the bastard had a dick in his pants. Cujo had left a scar though, and that wasn't easy to do to a shifter. We healed fast.

Cujo didn't shift. But I offered, and that was the best I could do. If I was an alpha—his alpha—maybe I could talk to him or possibly even force a shift. But I wasn't an alpha. I was an omega attempting to fill the role and save my family, and that's what all of them were: Family.

"What's that scent?" Lewis asked, scenting the air again, his twin doing the same. "It's off."

"That's why we're stopping. We're at the border of not one, but two packs. *If* I navigated us correctly, they're Greycoast and Northbay." And that was a big if. It wasn't as if we had a map of which territory belonged to which packs.

It was so easy to get off mark when traveling as long as we had, taking as many side trips away from people as we had, weaving in and out of the trees to avoid a direct path as often as we had. But I'd followed the stars, and based on the research I'd been able to do while "cleaning" the pack house, there were very few packs in this direction, this distance, that abutted the way these two did.

But still. Being wrong could lead to all kinds of badness.

"Niko, isn't that what we want?" Seymour asked. "They're our best hope. Kenon and Piers can't keep going like this." He let out a long breath and added so softly I barely heard, "I can't keep going like this."

"It is what we want. They're the only packs we have a shot with." Letting us onto their packlands for even a short time would put a huge ass target on their back and I hated that, but I didn't see any other option. "They're known to be kind, welcoming, and fierce."

Rumor had it they even took down a dark healer. But that wasn't what impressed me the most. It was the way Carter, the alpha—for he would never be *my* Alpha—talked about how weak they were, working together to protect their own. He saw that as the ultimate sign of patheticness. In Carter's mind they weren't strong enough and needed help.

That was where he was wrong. They were strong enough because they knew when they needed help.

Just like I knew we needed help, as much as I hated it.

But was this the help I needed, or would it put us

right back where we had been, only in a worse position—that of traitors?

Just then my brother answered the question I'd been too scared to answer for fear of messing everything up, in the worst way possible: he bent over, emptying the contents of his stomach onto the ground.

I rushed to his side, not touching him for fear of making it worse, wishing it was me and not him suffering so.

"He needs real food." Ralf placed a hand on my shoulder. "And a healer."

"So do I," Seymour's voice cracked. "I want to be strong. I am strong. But also… I'm so weak and when I'm weak…" He didn't need to say more; we all knew he wasn't getting enough nourishment for himself, much less his son.

"You are strong, Papa," Lewis assured him. "So much stronger than I."

They were all strong. They were survivors.

"Brother?" He'd stopped puking, but his body still convulsed like he was—not quite dry heaving, no choking at all—but his body…

"My stomach—it's not my stomach but it is. Like I have a charley horse but in my middle." He tried to push himself up and failed. "I just need a minute."

I couldn't tell if it was his stomach or where the bear

trap had snagged his foot the second night out that was causing his issues, but in any case… it was bad.

"Niko," Seymour whispered in my ear. "I think he's in labor."

He couldn't be in labor. He. Could. Not. He was only five months along. His baby—I couldn't even think about it.

"We need to ask for a healer, shelter, and food." It was the only way. Anything else would result in at least one death. We had to stop his labor.

They all agreed, even Cujo coming up and baring his neck to me. Kenon rode on his back, no harness. Just climbed on up there and Cujo didn't seem to mind.

"What do we do if the Shadowpine pack finds us?" We went through this every time we wore our skin. It was a routine by this point, but we couldn't take it for granted that we remembered the plan. It was life or death. One false move… I couldn't bring myself to think about it.

"Seymour?" I asked him first; his needs were different from the rest of us.

"I head to the largest body of humans I can get to. If I can find a homeless shelter, I go there. Tell them I've been abused and need safety. Humans have programs for that." I had no faith they were good, but it would be a place for him to start.

"Twins?"

"Stick together." They both said it at the same time. Ideally they would spread out, making it impossible for the Shadowpine pack to use their full man power on them. But that wasn't something they'd be able to do, and even *if* they were able to manage, they would be weaker for it. They needed to stay together.

"And find a city. Blend," Lewis added. There was no blending with those two, but they'd survive. I had to believe that.

I didn't ask Piers, grateful he was finally able to sit back against the tree. He would head toward people and find help. He was pregnant, and as much as I hated it, he'd find better help alone.

What they didn't know and I'd never tell them was that I wouldn't be headed towards people.

I would head straight towards Carter and I'd officially challenge him.

It wouldn't end well. I would lose. Of course I would. But the time it took to have a formal challenge would buy everyone else the time they needed to be safe.

"Cujo, you've got this." I nodded in his direction so he'd not feel excluded. I wasn't even sure the man was in there anymore. For all I knew he was all wolf. He mattered though, and I needed him to see that.

Seymour shifted.

"Which pack?" Lewis asked, as he grabbed the harness and affixed it to Seymour securely.

Cujo came over and nosed the harness. "I think Cujo wants to keep carrying Kenon," Ralf told his brother, who unharnessed Seymour.

"Shift Papa, let us know what you want for your son." Sometimes I sounded too much like an Alpha, capital A for my own liking.

He shifted, tilted his head to Cujo. "It would be an honor." Seymour was so weak.

Lewis picked up Kenon while this time his brother set up the harness. They had created it just for our escape. Genius.

They might think I was the leader, but we wouldn't be here if it wasn't for each and every one of us. We all played a part in each other's survival.

"Which pack?" Lewis asked again after Kenon was secure.

"To the south. I scent them closer and I don't think we have time." I wasn't sure we had the time either way, my brother very much not okay.

"Can you shift, my brother?" Piers nodded and took his fur, slow and lunky, but he got there. The shift looked painful, as fur erupted slowly on his arms and his limbs contorted with pops and cracks.

We all followed suit and started south, our steps, even Piers's, a little bit lighter knowing we'd reached a possible haven.

Not much lighter though, because as much as I'd like to believe the tales of these two packs, I couldn't trust any of it to be true.

Trust was for people who had nothing to lose, and we had everything to lose. We brought with us the next generation.

Chapter Three

Dylan

Darren was already sitting at the picnic table underneath the pavilion where I and my Betas always met for our meetings when I walked over. The budget analysis was done, thankfully; all I needed was for some of the elders in the pack to look it over, then perhaps it was time to begin the discussion on what business avenue to pursue next.

When I was a child chomping at the bit to become alpha one day, it never occurred to me just how much paperwork was involved. I'd thought being alpha meant being admired and respected by all. I hadn't realized it took a lot of work to earn that respect and even more to keep it. I loved it though, despite the struggles. I loved my pack and I took great pride in providing for them.

The gathering area we met under was built by my brother Ozzy and served as a place for the entire pack to convene for celebrations, pack runs, and regular meals. The poles holding up the pavilion were hand carved by Ozzy, depicting various scenes from our pack history, from when our pack first found this land, to the full harvest moon night when I was named alpha. His work was nothing short of a masterpiece.

The table that was mine unofficially served as a place for all pack members to go if they needed to speak with me for any reason. I liked to keep my Beta meetings out in the open so that I was approachable as a leader. It worked well for us, most of the time. Some days we had more interruptions than we could handle, and our meetings didn't accomplish much, but today seemed to be a slow day in the pack. Everyone was busy with their own tasks.

I sat down across from Darren. In the night since I'd last seen him, it seemed he'd gotten some rest and had a fresh shower. He looked slightly better than he had when I spoke with him that morning. The Beta role was looking good on him already.

"Have you had the pleasure of eating at the Pavilion Cafe?" I said, laughing at the name we had attributed to the restaurant-like set up we had.

He shook his head. "I have not."

"I don't think you have anything like this at Greycoast. It's pretty nifty, though. When my father was alpha, the pack numbers grew so fast that we couldn't build enough houses to keep up with the demand. So many of them were built small, without full-sized kitchens. That's when the restaurant idea was formed."

I gestured to the building to our left. It was a one story structure, nothing super special to look at, but inside was an industrial kitchen with a huge fridge, walk-in freezer, large grill, fryers, everything we needed to keep our pack well fed. Surrounding the restaurant was an elaborate garden and various greenhouses where we grew a lot of our own vegetables and herbs.

"It was meant to be a temporary solution, but the pack enjoyed having the shared kitchen so much that we've kept it. Now it operates very much like a restaurant. A few of our members have even gone away to school to become classically trained in culinary arts. It's run twenty-four hours a day and is staffed by pack members of all ages. We even have a manager." Even with our dwindling numbers, it was still a bustling venture and fostered pack bonding.

Darren's face told me that surprised him. "Wow," he said.

"Yeah, and the chef's mate went to school for hospitality. Running hotels and that kind of thing. She learned quite a few skills that actually came quite useful for how we manage our dorms and keep the restaurant flowing efficiently." My chest puffed with pride. The pavilion restaurant had begun under my dad, but had been expanded and perfected since I'd taken the role as Alpha. All my pack members came together to keep our pack happy and safe; there was no better feeling as an alpha than knowing that your pack was well cared for.

"That's great," Darren said. "Do many of the pack members go to college?"

"A few," I said. There was a delicate balance between sending everybody and sending only the right amount of people we needed to gain the education and return. It was rare for a wolf to leave a pack and want to stay in the human world; we were pack animals, after all. But finances became an issue, and wolves living outside their pack lands tended to become lonely and depressed. It was hard on them. "We're able to send more and more now that online school is becoming more popular. It's no less expensive, though."

My two Betas, Vaughn and Hutch, arrived. They bared their necks to me, then sat down at the table.

Vaughn and Hutch looked very much alike, almost like twins, but they were first cousins. Both were tall and muscular. They would fill the role of enforcer for me, should the need ever arise.

"Guys, this is Darren," I said. "He's going to be joining us as one of my Betas."

Hutch extended his hand and Darren shook it. Vaughn nodded his head. They'd known I was going to be asking someone to be a Beta, so this came as no surprise. Vaughn and Hutch had been my closest friends growing up. They'd always known they would be my Betas once I was alpha.

"What's on the menu today?" Vaughn asked, picking up the slip of paper that listed some of the meals available for ordering. There were a few dishes that they made no matter what. Steak being one of them, of course; we were wolves, after all. French fries were another because they were just delicious.

"Meatloaf, I think."

"Awesome. I've been craving Sarah's meatloaf," Vaughn said. Hutch hummed in agreement. It was amazing meatloaf.

"I don't think we have anything to discuss today," I said. "I just wanted to introduce everyone so we could get to know one another. Maybe we can eat together and just chat." I didn't want Darren to feel on the spot, but I also wanted him to feel like he belonged and was welcomed and not like I was shoving him at the other Betas.

"Alpha!" Ilyssa, one of our school teachers, came running toward us. Fear rolled off of her in waves and it set my wolf on edge. She was out of breath when she finally got to our table. She leaned against the edge as she took deep breaths. We all stood, my

Betas flanking my sides and looking around to see where the danger might be.

"What is it?" I asked. Blood pulsed through my veins and my wolf surfaced, ready to take on whatever threat arose.

"Intruders," she breathed. "In the north end of the forest, not far from the Greycoast border."

"Are they—"

She shook her head. "They're not members of Greycoast. They don't smell like them at all."

"How many?"

"Four or five. All omegas, I think. They don't look very good, but I couldn't see them very well. I came running as soon as they were spotted." She took in a breath. "I think—there was a child."

Odd. Intruders didn't usually come with children. They slowed things down and gave them a weakness. "Go secure the children, please. Let others know to be on alert."

I dashed toward the forest, my Betas flanking my side. My gut said they weren't a danger, not with a child, but I couldn't take a chance, not when it came to the lives of my pack. As soon as we reached the trees, we shifted to our wolf forms, leaving our clothes on the dirt floor of the forest's edge.

As if it was completely routine and normal for him,

Darren trailed behind me, while Vaughn and Hutch stayed at my side. The four of us ran in a diamond formation through the woods. I knew then that I had really made the right choice in asking Darren to join my Betas.

I scented a few other pack members of mine on the trail. Stewart, another of our teachers, and Chad, one of the younger alphas in our pack. They must've been out for an afternoon run when they'd come across the trespassers.

Given the seclusion of the forest, it was rare for anyone to stumble upon the territory accidentally; if they were here it was because they came here purposefully.

We reached a spot where Stewart and Chad were crouched behind a fallen log. Six other wolves were coming towards us, traipsing through the unfamiliar woods. They walked at a slow pace and crowded in with each other when we approached. In the center of their pack sat a small child in some sort of saddle. He couldn't have been much more than two. It was hard to tell with his ribs being so prominent, but he was definitely not a newborn.

They were scraggly, dirty, and completely underweight. All of them were omegas, like Ilyssa said, and they were in rough shape, even the child. Their fur was of varying colors, some grey, some dark black. One was almost completely white, though it was hard to tell from the dirt and grime that was matted to it. The smell of blood wafted over, both old and fresh, which meant one or more of them was injured and had been for a while.

Not sensing any danger from them, I shifted to my human form and my Betas followed suit, flanking my side.

"We mean you no harm," I said. My Betas stood at my side geared up for a fight, though appearing outwardly as relaxed. We didn't need to frighten the group in front of us.

Their scent was unfamiliar, and it was almost as if the group didn't belong to the same pack, their scents were so different. They clearly relied on and trusted each other though; the way they banded together, pushing the smallest of them into the center of a circle, they knew how to defend themselves. They weren't from around here, that was certain. The only packs here were Greycoast and Northbay, and we knew the Greycoast pack. My own brother was mated to one of the Betas there.

This group didn't smell like a threat. They were scared, running from something. How far behind were their pursuers?

The one in front shifted to his human form. The one next to him shifted shortly afterwards, his shift loud and clunky—as if it took great effort. The rest remained as wolves. The two men were both scrawny, but one had a protruding belly. A pregnant omega. Where was the alpha? My stomach clenched. Was that who they were running from?

My heart beat hard against my chest as I studied the one in front. He appeared as their leader, the others crowding behind him and watching for his signal, much like my Betas watched me for mine. Only unlike me, he wasn't an alpha.

His eyes were dark and focused on me like daggers. He was small, like most omegas, but he gave the vibe that he wouldn't back down from a fight. His ribs were visible, but somehow he spiked an arousal in me that was surprising and not welcome at a time like this.

"We'd like safe passage through your territory," the non-pregnant one said. His voice was strong and never wavered as he spoke.

"Who's asking?" I said.

"Why does it matter?" he retorted. He kept his chin high, giving no indication that he was going to bow down to me, alpha or not.

"Where have you come from?" I asked.

"That's not important. We just need safe passage through your territory. Perhaps we could stay a few nights in the woods and rest. We're not here to cause trouble."

I felt the presence of other pack members around us, though they hadn't shown their faces just yet. They were hidden in the woods, being nosy.

"Why don't you follow me back to my home? We can get you a hot meal. We have people who can help you," I offered. I lifted a hand and took a step closer.

"We don't need your charity," the leader bit out. "We just need to rest, and then we can work off the meal in trade." His breath came in heavy pants. He put on a fantastic show of bravery. Never before had I seen an omega stand up to an alpha like this.

It wasn't often that I had to dip into the power that an alpha had to make the wolves around him obey. But I did so now. "Come with me," I said, putting all the force that I had of an alpha into my voice.

The omegas in front of me were all unaffected. They didn't even waver, nor make any move to obey my command.

My Betas loosened their stance, confusion rolling off them. No matter who their allegiance was to, it was hard for a wolf to deny the command of an alpha, but they all were completely unaffected.

"Niko," the pregnant omega said, and he gripped his belly. "I need—" He collapsed to the forest floor with a thud.

"Reeva!" I shouted for our pack healer; they would

be able to help. I went to his side, kneeling in the dirt as I looked over the unconscious omega. I put a hand to his stomach and it was hard to the touch, like he was mid-contraction. His skin was ice cold. He was very much not okay.

Niko growled at me, but I ignored him. A pregnant omega needed help, so did the young boy and the rest of this ragtag group as well.

I wasn't going to let the grumpy one stop me.

My wolf, close to the unfamiliar omega for the first time, breathed in his scent and perked up.

Mate.

Chapter Four

Niko

"Niko, I need—" I'd been so focused on the Alpha and his Betas I failed to see just how distressed my brother was until he fell to the ground with a thud.

I dropped to the ground listening for his breathing. It was steady, his heart still thumping in his chest. That didn't make any of this okay, but it meant we had hope, we weren't too late. I could not lose my brother, he was my whole world.

The pack alpha rushed to my brother's side calling out for a Reeva or Reba; I wasn't even focusing enough to figure out which. My wolf wanted to tear through my skin and keep the Alpha from my brother, letting out a low growl of warning.

The Alpha meant him no harm. Person me could feel that. But my wolf wasn't taking any chances, instead growling at the alpha.

By some miracle, instead of bleeding me, the Alpha

gave me a look of sympathy and then went back to his task at hand, which included picking up my brother.

Ours, my wolf pounded at me. It took what little strength I had left to keep him at bay.

He's going to help.

"Tell Reeva to meet us at the infirmary," the Alpha barked at one of his Betas and then turned to me. "Tell your wolves to follow us."

He stepped around me and took long strides, my brother in his arms, carrying him to the infirmary as if he was pack and not some stranger breaching their borders.

"We are safer with him," I explained and jogged off after the Alpha, glad I could sense them all behind me.

The pack lands were much nicer than those we came from; clearly they took care of their land, nurtured it instead of depleting its resources and leaving it to rot. They didn't have the shacks for those that were kept in cages and beautiful cabins for those who were free. It all looked—even. Like they were all in the same boat together.

And that shouldn't have surprised me. I knew not all packs were like my birth pack and the Shadowpine pack. But still—seeing it somehow showed me it was real and not a fairytale my brother and I made up when things got bad. Not that we'd ever seen good times. Things had always been bad for us.

"Come right in, Alpha." A person a solid six inches shorter than the alpha stood at the door of a large cabin, the door wide open. "All of you as well." They directed the second part at me and the wolves and sweet Kenon.

The alpha took the steps two at a time, explaining to the person, who I now knew to be Reeva, what was happening. They scurried him into a room and I stood there unsure of what to do. Things were happening so quickly, and as much as I wanted to be there holding my brother's hand, I didn't want to get in the way and inadvertently endanger him more.

"Brother can come in or stay out, but there's no room for all of you. I will get to you all. I promise." Their calming voice had me believing them.

They had power to them—not dark power, the kind that was palpable and made your stomach turn just being in its presence. No. This was different and I couldn't quite put my finger on it. But it was good. Healing.

I looked to the crew, Kenon squirming to get out of his harness. "Can you shift?" I asked Seymour, whose body was sprawled out on the floor. He put his head down, his sad eyes looking at me.

"Don't worry. I got this, Papa." I went to Kenon and helped him out of the harness, holding him against my hip.

"Little wolf, we need to go check on my brother. Can you be really really quiet?" I asked, knowing he not only could, it was his nature. Watching your father get beaten unconscious because you cried will do that to a kid, and that wasn't even the worst thing he'd witnessed in his short time on this earth.

My heart bled for him—for all of them. Not one of them was unscathed by the hand fate dealt them. Not one.

We would make it through, though. We'd come too far not to. We were stronger than our past.

Kenon hugged me close as I walked to the small room. "May we come in?" I asked at the threshold, unsure what I would do if I was told we could not.

"You may." Reeva was rubbing some kind of oil on my brother's belly. I could scent some flowers, maybe curry? And something else… something woodsy. "Your brother is going to need some time with me. Is the young one sick?" They looked to Kenon.

"No, he just wanted to get off of Cujo and I didn't think this the best place for him to run around." My biggest worry wasn't that he would break things.

No, it was that he would hide. He was good at hiding and I hated the reasons why.

"Alpha, maybe they can go to the omega dorms and get food and showers. They look like they've been running for days." Reeva looked at me with questioning eyes. "Has he?" they asked, meaning my brother.

"Yes." Many, many days. "Weeks." Three. I hated to give ourselves away, but if the information was needed to help my brother, it was needed. He came first.

"Alpha, they will need food and meat… lots of meat, and this little one… he needs citrus."

"I'll arrange it." The Alpha held his hands out for Kenon.

Mine.

Well, that answered that. My wolf wasn't about to share, and honestly I wasn't sure I had the strength to keep him from taking control.

"Send one of the others in for him." I didn't even lower my head and pretend I wasn't taking his authority on this. So what if he was hot with sympathy in his eyes and a pack who didn't cower from him. He wasn't in charge of us, and if he was going to play that way we'd have to figure out a new plan—possibly heading to the Greycoast pack to seek help until my brother got back on his feet.

"Understood." And then he did something that shook me to my core—he bared his neck to me. Make no mistake about it, he was the big boss here, and if it came to his pack or us, we'd be put down so fast we wouldn't have a chance to blink. But in this—in me protecting Kenon—he was giving me the power.

Had we crossed the veil into a new realm? Because this sure as shit didn't feel like reality.

Ralf came in for Kenon and promised to keep an eye on everyone. I'd have given him more instructions, but just then my brother moaned, bringing me to the matter at hand.

I stepped closer, wanting to ask Reeva what they were doing to my brother and if he was going to be okay. I dared not ask. It felt like anything I did to distract Reeva's concentration could have the entire process crashing down like a house of cards. So instead I bit my tongue.

Reeva had moved on from the oil and now had their hands over my brother's abdomen almost, but not quite touching. Had it been anyone else I'd have questioned them, but with Reeva it meant something. I wasn't sure why I believed that, but I did.

"How far along?" They didn't look up from their spot.

"About five months, we think." That bastard had

been raping my brother for months and didn't stop once they discovered his pregnancy. Not that Carter would call it that. No. In his mind my brother was property, and he was doing what he was put on this earth for. Gods, I hated that man with every fiber of my being.

"Is the alpha father a wolf as well?"

"He's not the father," I barked back and then reeled it in. They were trying to help, and me not controlling my temper wasn't going to help. "I mean yes."

"He looks but a child." Reeva turned their head to the side and put their ear to my brother's belly.

"He is of age." We didn't need them to think we stole a youth. "He is twenty."

"Is that his boy you were holding?" Reeva picked their head up and put both their hands on my brother's left side. "The question is important."

I stopped staring and tried to remember the question. Oh yeah… "No. The boy's father was one of the wolves out there. They will need a healer too."

"You all will," Reeva said and turned from me and went to the counter.

"We think—is my brother in labor? It's too soon." I didn't know much about babies, but I knew that. Gestation was nine months, and while we could handle an early labor, five months was way too early. The child wouldn't survive.

"Yes on both accounts." They opened a cabinet door and took out a mortar and pestle. "And that is why I'm going to stop it. Sit in that chair. I may need more answers."

"I know I will." The alpha of the pack was back. "Keep your wolf at bay." His firm words meant business.

My wolf wasn't even that close to the surface. I mean he was, but the weeks of running had him too weak to break through without my help or a really strong need, such as protecting my brother or Kenon.

"He is." I didn't address his comment about having questions, instead ignoring it and asking my own."

"They are safe?"

"They are with Darren. Darren knows what it is like to be new here. He will make them feel as comfortable as could be expected given the situation… which is what, exactly?"

And circling it back to question time. Great.

"If you two are going to have a pissing match you can leave." Reeva turned around, a mug in their hand. "But this omega needs you so I suggest you reel it back." They gave us a very stern *don't try me* look.

"One of you two needs to help this man sit enough that we can get this tea in him. It is infused with a blend of herbs, and if I am correct and it is dehydration and lack of nutrition causing the labor, this will stop it while we remedy the root cause."

"I can help." The alpha took a step towards my brother.

Mine.

"I got it, alpha. He's my brother." I got up and behind my brother as fast as I could manage, which wasn't very.

"Dylan."

"No, his name is Piers," I corrected. I stood behind my brother, trying to figure out the best way to help him up. It was as if all my strength had been sucked from my body and my limbs weren't cooperating. Could I even lift him?

"My name is Dylan. How about we each take a side?" The alpha didn't move, as if waiting for me to decide… as if an omega's answers mattered.

I had no idea what to do with that. I was ready to pounce on him for trying to take control at every bend, but he wasn't… he saw me as… I didn't even know what, but not less than scum property, which was what I'd been used to for far too long.

"That might work." I stepped to the side.

With the two of us assisting him, we managed to get my brother in a semi-seated position. I wouldn't call him conscious, but he wasn't completely out either, and when Reeva brought the mug to his lips and encouraged him to sip slowly, he managed to get a few sips down before needing nudging again. Each drink was a bit longer than the one before, my brother a bit more awake and alert until the entire mug was empty.

"How are you feeling now?" Reeva asked him. "Ready enough for them to let you go or not just yet?"

"My pup?" His voice was hoarse, like he'd been screaming in agony. I hated that I knew that sound.

"Will be fine. It will just take some time." Reeva set the mug on the counter. "Can you sit on your own?"

"Sleep?"

"Yes, sweet omega. Sleep. Get rest for your baby." Reeva nodded to the alpha and I, and we gently lowered him down. "I'll get him a blanket."

Reeva went out and came back in almost immediately with a thick blanket they used to wrap my brother in and a pillow for under his head. "Sleep well, omega."

Reeva shooed us out of the room and followed us to the waiting area we had been in initially.

"Alpha, the newcomers will need to see me and they will need clothing. It's too chilly in the evenings this time of year."

And just like that, I became self-conscious of my nudity. Not that the alpha was any more dressed than I was. Unlike me, he was muscular, whereas I now resembled a skeleton more than the young man I was *before*. That's what I called our time pre-Shadowpine pack. Before.

"I will arrange it," he said.

Piers's moan came through the cracked door.

"I will attend to him." Reeva left the two of us standing there.

"Reeva is the best. Your brother couldn't be in better hands." Dylan started to take a step closer to me and stopped midway. "I would trust Reeva with my brother."

"We don't need clothes." Because that was the best response to his reassurance. "We will be leaving as soon as Piers wakes up." The longer we stayed here, the more riled up my wolf was getting. We needed to put more space between Shadowpine and us. How ridiculous I was to think we could stay here for even a few days!

Not ridiculous. Worn out beyond exhaustion.

"Your brother's in there needing our healer… let

him heal. Your pack needs to heal. You need to heal. All of you need rest." His words slammed into me. He was right. We did.

Mine.

This time the wolf wasn't talking about my brother or the other wolves. He was talking about Dylan or maybe the pack. How he longed to not be the one in control.

How I longed to be the one not in control—people counting on me—people needing me to be stronger than I was because if it wasn't me in the lead there would be no one.

They mistook my ability to take a beating and still not learn my lesson about cowering to Carter as a sign that I was strong.

I wasn't strong. I was terrified, but the fear of failing them was far deeper than the fear of my own death or worse—capture.

"It's not safe," I all but whispered, and he took a step closer, his body close enough I could feel his breath.

"It is safe. Of that I vow." I wanted to wrap my arms around him, feel his touch, his comfort. It was messed up. I couldn't show my weakness like that… not now.

"Only until the healer says we are strong enough to

travel. You don't deserve the… it's better if we leave." What was it about this man—this Alpha—that I almost told him too much. He was safer not knowing who was after us or why. We really were the equivalent of a target on his pack's back.

"You might not be an alpha, but you are their Alpha." He reached over and pulled a leaf from my hair, and for a split second I allowed myself to believe it was something more. I needed to quell that feeling. Hope, trust—those could be used against me and would only make the disappointment in the end more painful.

Accepting minimal help was one thing, wanting more—that was a hard nope.

"I will check on your wolves and the boy. You stay with your brother. He needs you. They all need you."

If only I were enough.

Chapter Five

Dylan

Leaving Niko and his brother in the infirmary was harder than it should have been. My wolf was reluctant to leave and whined with each step that I took as I walked away. It was the best place for them and still… my wolf wanted me there, protecting them.

The paths we'd forged around the makeshift village that we called our pack home were worn with use, trodden down to hard packed dirt. The center of our territory was really just a cluster of houses and buildings, most of them small in stature, carved out in the woods. Each building was well maintained and sturdy, despite their age. They weren't fancy and we didn't need them to be.

The oldest was my grandfather's house, the original alpha house, built over a hundred years ago. The newest was the infirmary. It had been another of my passion projects since becoming alpha. With more adult pack members than ever before, we needed a hospital-like setting to provide for their health needs. We had quicker healing abilities than humans, but we were still animals who had illnesses, broken bones, and cuts. We kept Reeva busy.

The pack seemed to be abuzz with activity. Many pack members were clustered in small groups, talking… or rather, gossiping. It wasn't every day that we rescued a band of omegas from the forest and gave them shelter. The pack was naturally curious and likely had the same questions about this group of omegas that I did.

What the hell were they running from? How long had they been out there on their own? I couldn't scent any lies on Niko, but then again I couldn't scent much besides fear. He had no reason to trust us, nor I him, and yet I did and so did my wolf.

The other omegas had been shuffled to the dorms, where I was headed now. There were four of them, and also the young child, Kenon. Each had been thin and scraggly, their eyes wide with fear. They all looked at the alphas like we were going to strike them at any moment. My heart broke and my wolf growled just imagining what had put the fear in their eyes. It had to have been far worse than anything I'd ever experienced if they were willing to flee with a pregnant omega and a child.

The omega dorms were a larger building that resembled more of a school house than anything else.

Inside was the common area, which had a living room set up. There were games, books, computers, and a television. Down each hallway was a set of rooms. Each floor had about five rooms and there were three floors total. They served as a safe space for unmated omegas in the pack to gather and hang out, and potentially live if they wanted their own space.

During my time as pack alpha, the omega dorms had remained mostly empty. Instead, we'd used it as a type of hoteling space for families between homes or for other shifters as they visited. We'd never had the amount of omegas that were in it now and if you had asked me yesterday, I'd have said it was a bad thing. But today—now that we needed it, I was glad for the space. There was no way these omegas would trust staying in the same space as others yet... maybe ever.

I pushed open the doors and sniffed, trying to determine where the omegas had been taken. I found Vaughn. He sat on the couch in the living room area, a bottle of water in his hands and a haunted expression on his face.

"Everything all right?" I asked.

He nodded, then grimaced and shook his head. "What the hell happened to them?" he asked, his voice raw and shaky. "I've never seen omegas in that state. Their fear... the air was so thick with it I nearly choked."

I sat down next to him, hating how accurate his description was. My muscles relaxed and an ache set in. "I don't know. Niko seems to be their leader and he wasn't overly forthcoming with information. Not that I blame him. I don't think they got to the state they were in on their own."

Vaughn winced. "They clearly have reason to distrust alphas. Ilyssa is helping them to get settled with food and clothes. They didn't seem to like being around me."

"Ilyssa has the school teacher vibe," I said, hoping to make him a bit less self-conscious.

I knew that no matter his size or stature he would have intimidated them simply because he was an alpha under normal circumstances. But Vaughn was of the larger sort. He was my Beta, and more specifically, my enforcer, should I ever need one. He and Hutch both were larger wolves, bigger than even me. He was intimidating even without the past they were running from.

"Where do you think they came from? Any clues that you gathered?" I asked. Niko had been less than forthcoming, but I'd been directly asking him questions. My hope was that in conversation with each other, the rest of his makeshift pack might've let some things slip out. If it was just privacy, I wouldn't need to know. But this wasn't that. There was danger involved and as Alpha, my best way to protect them was to know what I was protecting them from.

Vaughn shook his head. "They're scared. Terrified of the slightest movement. One of them won't even shift. He was still in his wolf form when I came out here." He inhaled deeply, letting it out slowly. "They have a child with them, but the kid wouldn't look at me. He seemed listless. Ilyssa is checking if he needs medical attention. Someone hurt them all. Badly." He rolled his shoulders back. "Makes my wolf restless seeing them like that."

Mine too.

"Kenon is the child's name. Reeva will be around later, once Piers is stable. They will see to any medical needs." Of which I imagined there were many.

"Piers is the pregnant one?" I nodded. "Will he… will he be okay?"

My gut tightened. "I sure hope so. He was able to drink, and Reeva seemed optimistic. I'll get a full report later, but if anyone can help him, it's Reeva."

I had my theories on how they all got to that state, but wasn't ready to voice them out loud. I hated that they might be close to the truth, or worse—that my theories might be too tame for what had actually happened to them. I didn't enjoy the thoughts racing through my mind on what could have been. Instead, I just let Vaughn talk.

"I've heard rumors, you know? Every so often my brother visits—he went to the Marblefalls pack, after he met his mate there."

I nodded. I knew Vaughn's history; obviously as alpha it was my business to know much of the family history of pack members.

"Do you think there really are packs out there that keep omegas like slaves? In cages and shit? They keep them locked up for breeding. They… beat them to get them to obey. Certainly seems the case with this group." He spoke really quickly and in a whisper as if saying it out loud made it real.

My stomach rolled. "That would make sense." And explained why they didn't smell like they were from the same pack. If you owned someone, you didn't make them one of you. I hated how accurate I suspected his conjecture was.

"Maybe they escaped a situation like that," I continued, careful to keep my voice even. "My line of thinking is similar. Someone or something or a group of someones kept these omegas in the condition they were in." I doubted that they all just picked up and left a perfectly safe pack one day to wander along on their own, especially not with one of them being pregnant.

"How old would you say is the child they had with them?" I asked. I needed any clue about how long these omegas had been in this condition. Then again, without hearing it directly from one of them, I would just be guessing.

"I'm not sure," Vaughn said. "The omega was holding him pretty close. I couldn't get a good look. Couldn't be more than three years old. But it's hard to tell since he's probably malnourished. Hell, he could be ten for all I know."

"Fuck," I said and ran a hand through my hair. I preferred to gather all the facts before acting. I wasn't an impulsive alpha. This not knowing was driving me insane.

"You're going to let them stay, right boss?" The rawness of his emotion had it coming out as almost a plea. He'd spent less than an hour with these omegas and he already was as protective of them as he would be of one of our own—possibly more so. I got it. I really did. I was struggling with similar feelings.

I nodded. "Of course. If they want to." My wolf growled. *Mine.* No way in hell were we letting this group go. They might not know it, but they were pack now. "Niko doesn't want to stay. He doesn't trust us." And I wasn't sure it was that he didn't want to stay as much as he was terrified to.

"Is he the leader?" Vaughn asked.

"Seems to be," I said. The others had looked up to him, and his brother did as well, more than just as a big brother. Niko had obviously been the one making the decisions for them. He was their Alpha in that sense.

Vaughn smirked. "I've never seen an omega like that. Taking charge and challenging an alpha. Damn." There was a bit of pride in his comment.

My wolf preened as if pleased. Hearing the praise for Niko made him happy, even if the praise was about how he'd put me in my place.

Mate.

I bit back a groan. If my wolf was right, and Niko was ours, now was not the right time for that shit. Niko needed help, safety, and security. Not an alpha sniffing around looking to claim him. I needed a mate that would help me keep the pack strong and centered, not one that challenged my every word. We weren't mates.

Probably.

Maybe.

No, we weren't. My wolf was wrong and just being protective. It was his way.

"I can't say that I have either. He is strong. I'll give him that." Something had made that omega so daring, so strong, so committed to the omegas around him that he had become a pseudo alpha in the process. Whatever it was wasn't going to be allowed to hurt him again. "They can stay for as long as they need to. And if whatever is chasing them, whatever caused them to be in the state they're in, comes looking for them, we'll be ready." And I'd see them take their last breath. No omega should go through what they did. I didn't even know what it was, but anything that left them that scared, that fearful, that untrusting was something that needed retribution in the way of our ancestors… in blood.

No way was I letting anyone or anything near Niko and the omegas he protected. They were under my protection now. They'd only been here for a short amount of time, but as much as I tried to deny it, my wolf was right. He'd claimed them as his own—as our own. His loyalty was oddly centered on the omega leader of the group. Even if he wasn't ours and even if we could never claim him and even if he could never truly be ours, it was our duty to keep him safe to give him the best chance at a happy life.

My wolf thought of Niko as ours already. My wolf howled at the thought.

Mate.

I shook that thought away. No way. Now was not the time. There were more important things at hand—seven of them and an unborn babe.

Chapter Six

Niko

Every bone in my body ached. Every. Last. One.

I'd spent the night by Piers's side, dozing on and off again in the hard chair. I thought about taking my fur and curling up on the floor, but if he needed me, I wasn't sure how quickly I could shift back. The exhaustion was hitting me hard now that we'd stopped, as if my body took that as a sign we could rest.

Reeva had been amazing. I wasn't sure what herbs or whatever they put in the tea, but my brother was visibly doing better. Reeva had even been able to get him to eat a decent meal. Nothing fancy or too filling: a soup made with ground meats, rice, and some vegetables. A complete meal in a mug. For me it came with a sandwich on the side, but Reeva warned against him eating too much, saying the soup was what he needed for the moment.

And then Piers slept. He crashed hard, and had I not eaten the same soup as he, I'd have assumed there were some medicinal qualities to it to foster the sleep he needed. Reeva came in and out throughout the night checking on him and offering me a bed. I refused. I needed to be there to protect him if things should go awry.

And it wasn't even the Northbay pack that had me on alert. If anything, they soothed me—gave me the ability to breathe for the first time in I didn't know how long.

That didn't mean Carter and his crew weren't close by. It had been a miracle they hadn't caught us already. I'd seen what happened to omegas who tried to escape and wouldn't wish it on my worst enemy. Then again, I did wish that Carter and the rest of Shadowpine alphas received the same treatment they had inflicted on so many omegas.

I stood up as quietly as I could, the chair creaking slightly. I didn't want to wake Piers up, but I also couldn't stay as I was any longer. I felt like a man triple my age after completing a triathlon I hadn't trained for. Everything hurt. Every. Last. Thing. Even my toes ached when I wiggled them.

Taking in a deep yawn, I stretched, attempting to loosen up some of my muscles. I failed. They were stiff as a board.

I needed to check on the others, but I also needed to

stay with my brother. How did pack Alphas, the kind like Dylan, not the kind like Carter, do this all the time—figure out what priority they needed to focus on first when everything was a priority? The guilt of leaving the rest of them alone to stay with Piers had my mind racing for a better solution. Maybe Piers would wake up and be right as rain.

Watching his sleeping form, I recognized that as the fantasy that it was. His eyes were so sunken in, the coloring still off. He might be better enough to travel, but there was no miraculous recovery from anything I could see or hear.

"You staring at me?" Piers said, his eyes still closed. "Because if you have pity in your eyes I'll need to get off this bed and deck you, and I'm really too tired for that."

There was strength in his voice. Not a lot, but so much more than yesterday.

"I'm not looking at you with pity. Promise." I started to walk, no longer afraid I'd wake him up. "Besides, you don't have it in you to strike another person." Not my brother Piers; he was as good as they came.

"I'll make an exception, just this once." Piers cracked his eyes open and instantly shut them again. "Turn the light off?"

It wasn't on. "I can shut the curtains better." It was

all I could offer. The sun wasn't even fully up yet. If I were to guess it wasn't yet six.

"It's daylight?" He started to sit and gave up. "I think I'll ease into things." He sighed. "I feel so much better but also not. Like I took a nap when I needed a week's worth of sleep."

I messed with the curtains until they were as closed as they could be. "Probably accurate, only it was a long nap and you need a month's worth of sleep." A month we didn't have. "Want me to help you up?"

"Naw. I got it." And that time he did… barely. He twisted himself around so his feet dangled over the side. "I think Reeva's tea worked." His hands settled on his middle. "That was too close, brother."

"It was." Had we not stopped… I couldn't even bring myself to think about that.

"I need to stay here. If I have any hope of being able to keep my baby safe." He pushed himself off the bed, his feet landing on the floor with a thud. "I think they will let me—let us."

His knees started to give and I lunged forward to catch him. I was too slow, my reflexes too weak, and he landed on his ass. At least it wasn't his belly.

"I'm okay. I'm okay." I wasn't sure if he was talking to me or himself.

I helped him back up and onto the bed. "Maybe rest

a bit more."

"We have to ask them if we can stay. They aren't like Shadowpine and I can't keep doing this." He reached for the blanket, his body shivering with the cold that wasn't there.

"It's not an option. We're sitting ducks here." Which meant every hour we stayed increased the danger for everyone else in this pack.

"And if I go, I have no hope—my baby has no hope. I almost… I can't even say it."

I helped tuck him in, hating how cold he was. "You can bring the others if you need to. I'd understand."

"Not. An. Option." We were all going, or all staying. Divided we would perish. Even if we were safer apart, I wasn't leaving my brother and the other omegas I now thought of as family.

"They are good here. I feel it," Piers said.

"We will stay until I can figure things out," I reassured him. He needed his sleep, not worrying about the rest of this. That was my job. "I'm going to grab you another blanket."

I stepped into the next room and there was a pile of blankets. Reeva must have laid them there in case we needed them. Relieved I didn't need to go far, I hurried back in and covered him up. "Sleep, my brother. I will be in the chair when you awake."

And back into the chair I went. Reeva would be back soon enough to check on him, and his shivering had already subsided. I closed my eyes for just a second only to wake up to the scent of Dylan in the room.

I snapped awake, my wolf instantly alert.

Mine, he clawed at me.

Yes, yours. He was so protective of Piers… as was I. He still needed to cut that possessive shit down because holding him back was becoming increasingly challenging.

"Come." One word. Did he really think I'd respond to a command like that? Obviously he did, because next thing I knew he was walking out, my eyes glued to his ass. This was not the time nor the place for that, and Dylan was most definitely not the person for it.

Reeva came in with a tray of food and a pot of tea on it. "Hurry so you know how to get there," they insisted. "I've got your brother. He will be safe. I vow it." Reeva bared their neck to me.

"He was very cold." I indicated the blankets.

"That is why I left the blankets. Shoo." Reeva pointed to the door.

I found myself doing exactly that… rushing after the Alpha who had already made it out the door.

"You weren't going to wait?"

"There was no need." He slowed his steps. "We're going to my house—it doubles as the pack house."

"Are my people there?" I didn't dare call them pack, although they were. He'd have already scented out that we weren't from the same pack. Shadowpine owned us, but we were not their pack and they never pretended otherwise. We were their property.

"Keep up." He started walking faster, not racing, but at a normal pace, and my body cried from the exhaustion. Maybe a night in my fur would help.

We meandered through the village, most definitely taking the long way, and the entire time he pointed things out as if he were a tour director and not the Alpha who held our future in his hands.

"This is the pack house. It's also mine." We stopped at the path to his front door. "Be my guest."

Odd words from the man who insisted on my presence.

"Okay." I followed him in. I half expected there to be others there both from my group and his own. But there wasn't. Instead the house was vacant, the only scents those of a meal cooking.

"It smells delicious." My stomach added its two cents to the mix.

"There's a pot roast and potatoes in the crock pot.

Let's eat." I followed him through what I believed to be the communal room and into a large kitchen. "I made it myself. It's not fancy, but it will be good."

He took out two plates and handed me one. "Take all you'd like. This is all for us." A few minutes later we were at his table, our plates high, a tray of biscuits between us.

"If you don't like it, I have sandwich fixings," he offered as he took his second forkful and I still had not taken my first. "It's all from the same pot."

Great. He thought I was thinking he'd poison me when all I was doing was trying to form the words that needed to be said.

"Where are my wolves?" So much for me forming my thoughts carefully. I shoved a forkful of food into my mouth in some pathetic attempt to show my trust. My tastebuds were overloaded with the herbs and spices that flavored the roast. We'd had nothing but fresh kill while on the run, and while we were prisoners, Shadowpine had only allowed us stale bread and water most meals. Protein only when our bodies were starved for it. I'd never experienced flavor like this and it made my eyes water.

"They're in the omega dorms, and I'll take you there after dinner if you so wish." He snatched a biscuit, tore it in half, and dunked it into some of the juices. "They're fine. Reeva came over and checked them out once things with your brother looked good. They have food, clothing, and shelter."

I took another hunk of meat and jammed it into my mouth, chewing it slowly to buy me time.

"Your omega dorms are for pack omegas? Normally, I mean. But for omegas that are part of your *pack?*" I asked. Dylan didn't come across as a slave holding alpha type, but based on the enormous omega trade that was apparently out there, I had to be sure.

"The omega dorms are basically single housing for omegas. The name is antiquated, but the spirit of it is basically safe boarding house style living. It's not forced on omegas. It's an option for them." He pushed the biscuit tray closer to me. "Our pack has few omegas, and it was currently vacant if you were worried about that."

It sounded reasonable. I hadn't come from a pack that had one, but then again we were either mated or sold so there was no need, I supposed.

"They're scared?" I asked. Of course they were. "That was a dumb question. Ignore it."

I grabbed a biscuit.

"The fear rolling off them is significantly less than when I first met them. They're more worried about Piers than anything else."

That I believed. We'd wanted to go for so long, but it wasn't until things developed with Piers that we finally made the decision to do so. It was one thing to deal with the hell that was your life, but to allow it for Piers? None of us could do that. He was the shiny to our world, our eternal optimist and bright spot. Even now he saw this new pack as nice whereas I saw them as a potential threat. Piers was the best of us.

"That's good. My brother... he is almost able to travel. May we stay a day or two?" I bared my neck, letting him know we would accept his authority while we were here without saying the words.

"Reeva thinks it will be longer than that." He picked up a potato with his fork. "You will stay until it is safe."

"You are not my Alpha," I reminded him. "You are not any of ours."

Mine. My wolf needed to butt out.

"You're on my packlands. You need my help. I wish to provide it with no need of repayment. Don't split hairs about the terminology. I am the Alpha of this pack and you are here. We can keep you safe." Of course he had to go sound all logical.

"I don't know if anyone can." It slipped out and I hated myself for it. I stared at my half-empty plate. My stomach turned and I hoped I wouldn't lose the most delicious meal I'd had in my life.

"You will need to tell me everything sooner rather than later for the good of your pack, but I will let it go for now."

Mine, my wolf growled, my body starting to agree with him, my cock stirring at the most inopportune of times. Maybe it was the food. It couldn't be the alpha across from me, I refused to entertain that idea.

"We will stay until Piers is healthy enough to travel. But I have conditions." Like I had room to demand anything. "No one but us in the dorms."

"Done, with the exception of the Betas, and they can stay outside unless you invite them in."

"I'm serious. They can't have alphas sniffing around. It… it's important." I lowered my eyes toward my plate, not wanting to have to go any deeper than that.

"Agreed and also—that goes back to the I need to know what's going on thing. I need—my wolf needs to protect you." He rubbed his eye with the heel of his hand.

I wanted to roll my eyes, but I knew how alphas were. My wolf would do anything to protect the wolves in my care, and Dylan's wolf must feel the same way. "And I need to protect them."

"Fair enough. But when I have earned your trust..."

"I will tell you everything." It was an easy promise to make because he wouldn't earn that trust. No alpha would. Not ever.

Chapter Seven

Dylan

The word about our pseudo pack of omegas passed through the pack quickly in a buzz of excitement. There was a group of unmated omegas in the pack, and everyone was talking about it. Rumors of where they came from, what brought them here, and how long they were staying had begun. I'd even received a call from my brother and the alpha of Greycoast asking me about the situation. I'd informed them of what little knowledge I had, but there wasn't much to tell. I barely knew anything about Niko and his group. Just that they needed help.

I almost asked Byrom about how he knew that Cord was his mate when they met, but I decided against it. My wolf had been quiet about Niko for the past few days, and I hoped he would stay that way.

Ilyssa, Stewart, and Reeva were given the task of keeping the gossip within the pack to a minimum. It was fine to be excited and curious, but we had to be factual.

One of the omega pack members—Cujo was what the omegas called him—never shifted from his wolf form. I wasn't sure if the other omegas had ever seen him in his human skin. He could be seen walking around more often than the others. He seemed to be comfortable walking among us by himself. The others would go outside the omega dorms, but only as a group. Seymour and Ralf had eaten dinner at the pavilion together, and Lewis and Ralf had made a trip to the gardens to see the flowers.

Niko walked from the dorms to visit his brother at the infirmary, but only ever in his wolf form. I assumed once he was inside, he shifted, but I hadn't seen his human form for days. I missed it.

Everyone in my pack gave them all a wide berth under my direct order. The omegas were not to be courted in any shape or form. They were here to heal for however long they needed. They didn't need a bunch of horny alphas sniffing around them. Not that I would expect that from my pack, but Niko had been adamant about it and I was true to my word.

Since I had a free afternoon, where I wasn't expected to be anywhere, I took a walk to the infirmary to visit with Reeva. They might have an update on our patient. I knew that Piers's contractions had stopped and it seemed that his baby was doing just fine, but he was still staying where Reeva could keep a close eye on him.

Once I was inside the building, I sniffed and determined that Reeva was inside, as well as two others: Piers and Niko.

Reeva was a certified nurse, but maintained the role as pack healer, and they were damned good at their job. Had we had the time to spare them from the pack, we would have sent them to full medical school, but we couldn't afford to have them away from the pack for that long, nor did we have the funds.

In addition to having training on human medical care, they also knew of our more traditional healing methods. They and Greycoast's pack healer met regularly to trade remedies and discuss any cases that might need a second set of eyes. It was another way our alliance with the Greycoast wolves benefitted us both.

They looked at me from over their glasses as they sat at their desk. Their hair was pulled back in a tight braid. "To what do we owe this surprise visit, alpha?"

"Just checking in on our patient," I said.

"He's doing well. He has a lot better manners than some of the wolves around here, let me tell you." Reeva eyed me from over their glasses. "His brother is in there right now, if you'd like to visit."

"I don't want to intrude," I said. Though my wolf liked the idea of seeing Niko. We had half-way hoped that he would be here.

"You're not," Piers's voice sing-songed from down the hallway.

I chuckled and couldn't help but grin.

Piers, though he looked very much like his brother, had a night and day different personality from his sibling. He seemed more trusting and more inclined to smile and laugh with those around him. Despite the circumstances that put him in this position, his sunshiney personality shone through the storm clouds.

I walked down the hall toward his room and leaned against the doorframe, not bothering to step inside the small area. I didn't want to crowd the two omegas. We had an elaborate hospital set up, including an IV and electronic vital signs monitor, and both were hooked up to the omega. I couldn't remember the last time we'd needed to use it. And at first Reeva thought Piers wouldn't need it, but after he collapsed not one, but two times the next day, Reeva added a more human approach to his care. He was getting the best of both worlds.

We believed in being prepared, rather having too much equipment and not needing it, than needing it and not having it. Right now—we needed it and I hated that. But he was doing better. Not great, but better. So much so that Reeva was confident in his full recovery and the health of his baby.

"How are you doing, Piers?" I asked.

"I'm fine, Alpha. Thank you for asking. Reeva thinks that I might be able to move to the dorm soon." He grinned widely and his cheeks were full of color. HIs eyes even had a sparkle to them that I hadn't seen yet.

"Maybe!" they shouted from down the hall.

Wolf hearing. We learned to live with it. And love it or hate it, depending on the situation.

"Well, you're welcome to stay here at the infirmary for as long as you need to. There's absolutely no rush. We just want you and your baby to be healthy." The last thing he needed to do was rush out and slow his recovery. I trusted Reeva to make the right decision, but I also understood Piers's desire to be back with his wolves.

He nodded, a tinge of red spreading across his cheeks. "Thank you, alpha." His neck tilted as if he might bear his neck in submission, but then stopped. He rubbed a hand absently over his swollen belly. He'd told us he was about five months along, though he looked to be less than that, likely due to not eating well. In just the few short days that he'd been here, though, his health had improved considerably, which meant the baby's health had as well.

Niko pushed himself into a standing position. Now that he'd had a shower and was clean, his natural scent hit me like a ton of bricks and went straight to my groin. Jasmine. How was it that he had the rich, sweet scent of a flower I'd rarely seen? Nevertheless, there it was, and I wanted to soak myself in it. I clenched my jaw to keep from inhaling deeply and closing my eyes to savor the scent.

Damn, this omega was tempting and incredibly sexy with his slender, but still muscular build. He bowed to no man, no wolf, and I found it sexy as hell. All my life I assumed that I'd have an omega that would cater to my every need, like my omega father did to my alpha father.

But this? Standing on equal footing with an omega did things to me that I didn't even recognize. I clamped all those feelings down, locked them into a box, and buried them where I couldn't find them anymore. This omega was not mine. He was not for me. He'd been through something traumatic and he needed time to heal from that.

I needed an omega that would help me to lead the pack, not form one of his own.

It would never work between us.

Even if I wanted it to.

Which I didn't.

Mate. My wolf ignored my denial.

"I'm going to go hunting," Niko said.

My brow furrowed. "Hunting? We have a team of alphas that do that for us if we ever need game. If there's something you need, feel free to let us know and they will get it for you."

A growl rumbled from Niko's chest and Piers looked between us as if a fight might break out. My wolf didn't like a challenge from anyone, but was oddly quiet when it was Niko growling at me.

"I take care of my own and I'll hunt if I want to. Is that okay with you, alpha?" He said the word as if it was a swear word that made his tongue ache.

"Fine by me," I said. "Have at it. Please don't waste any. Eat your fill, but bring the carcass back to the pack. We'll utilize whatever pieces we can." I wasn't here to argue with my guest, and if he wanted to be blatantly disrespectful to me, I wasn't going to stop him. As long as he knew his place when we were amongst my Betas or the rest of the pack we wouldn't have a problem.

He nodded. "Thank you," he said in the barest of whispers.

I smiled at Piers. "Get some rest, okay? You'll be

back on your feet causing trouble in no time."

"Yes, alpha." This time Piers did bare his neck in submission to me. Interesting.

Once I was outside in the fresh air I found that I missed Niko's scent. My wolf immediately began searching for it. I caught his trail and my feet took me there without my brain's permission.

Niko was just in sight, jogging toward the woods. It didn't appear that he noticed me following.

I had things I could do, pack members I could visit, paperwork I could take care of. It had been a few days since I'd spoken to my grandfather. Perhaps today would be a good day to visit him. But instead, my gaze lingered on the woods where Niko had just disappeared. There was plenty of small game out there for a wolf like him to hunt. Rabbit, squirrel, maybe a fox if he was quick enough. How much of his desire to hunt was just his wolf wanting to stretch his legs? Or was he convinced he needed to provide sustenance to his pack? It stung my alpha pride that he didn't trust me to be able to provide for them, but I also respected him for it. A good leader never let their pack go without, not if they could help it.

Before I knew it, I was stripping my clothes, leaving them in a pile outside the infirmary and shifting into my wolf form. My wolf immediately followed the scent that Niko had left. Tracking prey was something that I was particularly skilled at. Aside from Hutch, I might be the most skilled tracker we had in the pack, so finding Niko was easy. I had a feeling my wolf would be able to scent him no matter the circumstances or how old the trail was. We would find our omega.

I kept my distance from him, only catching sight of him every so often. My grey fur lent itself well to camouflaging into the background of the woods. The wind was with me as well, so I was able to watch as Niko stalked a rabbit for a while, then took it down swiftly without remorse.

It seemed our omega was an extremely skilled hunter as well as leader. What other skills was he hiding beneath that tough exterior? And what would it take to get beneath it? What layers would reveal themselves if only he opened himself up to me?

I clenched my jaw, an action that in wolf form made me look more constipated than annoyed. I had no business sniffing around Niko when I had other issues to contend with. My pack had its own set of problems, and though my wolf wanted Niko as our mate, it wasn't in the cards right now.

The omega had clearly been through so much, and there I was, thinking of adding a relationship to the mix. Not only that, but a mating with me meant he'd be the Alpha Omega, a role in the pack that came with a unique set of challenges.

I still didn't know where the alpha was that had impregnated his brother or who he was and what the group of omegas had been through. I hadn't gotten close enough to any of the omegas to see if any of them smelled like they had a mate or to see a claiming bite. Piers didn’t have one, neither did Niko. Whoever they had all been with, whoever had had them under lock and key was not their alpha. Not in an official capacity that our wolves recognized.

My mind had wandered so much that I had lost sight of my omega. I sniffed the air, hoping to scent him. I did, but it was too late. A solid body of fur landed on my back and bit into my neck with a ferocious snarl. Enough that I felt the teeth, but not enough that I didn't realize it was a small bite devoid of malice. Niko was playing with me.

I rolled until Niko was thrown off of me.

He slid on his side across the forest floor, then got back up, shook until his fur fluffed out, and bared his teeth. His tail wagged, telling me that he was in a playful, not serious, mood.

I pinned my ears back and gave chase, launching myself toward him. He feinted in the other direction, and instead, I landed nose first into a pile of leaves. I swept the dirt from my snout, and leapt after him. He was quick, launching himself over branches and kicking off tree trunks to dodge my every attack.

Eventually, I was able to grab hold of his back leg and drag him down, careful not to inflict any wounds. He wiggled out of my attack easy enough, until he went on the defense. We wrestled until he had me pinned to the ground. I gave up the fight then, because I liked the feeling of him on top of me too much. More than I should have.

He sat back on his haunches, panting. He was out of shape. Though he was incredibly strong and agile for his size, he didn't have the stamina that a well-fed, well-rested wolf would have. Five days of solid meals had helped, but he had a way to go before he was at full strength.

I yipped and gestured for him to follow.

He did, and I led him to one of my favorite spots. It was deep in our territory, away from the edges so most outsiders didn't even know it was there. Within a few minutes, we were in a clearing that opened up to a special place within our territory. Our hot springs. The water bubbled and steam rose from the surface.

I shifted to my human form and ran and jumped into the water. I resurfaced and tossed my hair back.

"Come on!" I said. "It's fun."

He looked skeptical, his wolf face tilted in confusion, but he shifted and stood at the water's edge. He dipped in a toe and gasped.

"It's warm."

"It is," I said. "It's like a bath."

"I've never had a bath," he replied before taking one step into the shallow end. After a couple of steps he was fully submerged, the water coming up to his neck.

I was glad to see it. His nakedness was far too much of a distraction. Thankfully, my nether regions were covered and the wind was still on my side. Niko didn't need the smell of arousal and a hard cock in his face.

He needed caring. He needed pampering. He needed to learn to have fun and relax, even if it was just a temporary relief from the troubles that plagued him.

He needed to experience a bath. I ached to ask how it was that he'd never indulged in one before now. I'd heard some packs didn't utilize human things like indoor plumbing and electricity—was his pack one of those?

I wanted nothing more than to take him in my arms and tell him that he didn't have to be so strong all the time, that everything would be okay, I was here for him. Oddly enough, I longed to hear those exact same words from him. Together, he and I could support each other.

Chapter Eight

Niko

Eight days Piers had been in the infirmary. Eight days. I'd thought the first night had been the worst, seeing him so weak and in pain. But then I left him to deal with Dylan only to return and discover he'd gotten so much worse he was attached to human machines. Human. I didn't even know what they all did. Reeva tried to explain it to me, but my mind wouldn't allow me to fully take it all in. Every part of me focused on my brother, wishing I could give him my strength.

The first day I could breathe after that, Dylan came to visit, which he did often. But that time my wolf couldn't take it. He needed out… somehow leading us into a game of chase and frolicking in the water.

I needed that. Gods, how I needed it. I wanted to thank him for it, but it felt weird as we parted ways that night and since then—nothing. He hadn't stopped by the infirmary at all and I wasn't sure what to make of that.

He was the alpha of the pack. That came with responsibilities, and of course that meant he was busy. But he had been busy before—before we played as equals.

Maybe it was my stupid hard on that kept him at bay. And fair enough. I'd made it abundantly clear that alphas needed to give us a wide berth. He was no exception to that rule, and if he thought that he crossed a line or—shit—it was me that crossed the line.

Not that any of that mattered. What mattered was my brother getting all the tubes and monitors taken off of him and being able to join us in the dorms. *Dorms*—what a weird word for it. I couldn't wait to have us all together again at night. We'd all sleep better with us not being divided.

"I really haven't been putting anything in the IVs the past couple of days," Reeva explained. "I just kept them open in case I needed quick access. Their removal only means you will have better mobility and probably should increase your water consumption."

Reeva had been giving him more water than I drank in a week each day. I couldn't imagine more. But then again, I wasn't the one growing a pup. He was drinking for two.

"And this next part is going to make you mad." Reeva ripped off the tape, Piers flinching.

"It's done, though." Always looking on the bright side. "I'm not mad."

"That wasn't what was going to make you mad… I need you not to shift until I tell you you're in the clear." My brother looked up at them, his eyes wide with horror. "If you promise me that, I can let you go with your brother to be with your family." My brother just stared up at Reeva. "If not, I will need to be the asshat who demands you stay here."

Note to self—don't fuck with Reeva. They play hardball.

"Promise them, Piers." This was not about control; I scented the tinge of fear on Reeva when they mentioned my brother's shifting. It was for either his or his baby's well-being or possibly both.

"I'll do whatever it takes to keep my baby safe." He bared his neck to Reeva. "My silence was just me ingesting it all—not defiance." He looked to me. "You're thinking of my brother." He forced a chuckle as did I.

I mean—he wasn't wrong.

"Then go. Be with your family." That wasn't the first time Reeva called our motley crew family and I appreciated it. It meant they understood how important each and every one of them was to me and to each other. "I want you to check in with me in the morning." Reeva stood to the side, giving my brother room to get off the bed. "And drink your water." They handed him a large water bottle with markings on the side. "Drink three of these a day."

"I'll make sure he's here in the morning." I hugged my brother, so relieved he was over the hump enough to get out of this place and back with us.

We promised all the things that needed promising and took the papers, explaining everything we had promised. A half hour later we were on our way to the dorms.

"This place is nice," Piers said as we approached the building. "I had a picture of… never mind. It's nice." He didn't need to say what he had a picture of in his mind. I'd been with him in holding and transfer at Shadowpine. I knew right where his thoughts went and it was a dark place—the antithesis of this one.

"Yeah it is, and nothing like that. We will never be anywhere like that again." I wasn't sure if he meant the "holding house" or the "storefront" or any of the other awful communal places we'd been kept in over the years, but it was true for all of them.

"Let's get you a shower and a change of clothes. We have a pack meeting we're obligated to attend." He didn't even flinch at that. He took Reeva and

Dylan's kindness as a sign that the entire pack supported us. He always did look on the bright side of things.

The others? They more than flinched. I didn't blame them. Everyone they had met was wonderful, but they were only a fraction of the pack.

Darren promised us it was going to be a meet and greet type thing, not much more. He had been with us at the dorms quite a bit, protecting us, answering questions, and even playing with Kenon. Not once did he act like an alpha on the prowl, and being new to the pack, he had a perspective we appreciated.

The meeting was still a pack meeting—the entire pack and one we didn't belong to.

After a few hugs, a shower, and a pep talk, I led my brother and the entire crew to the meeting spot. How different it was from the Shadowpine pack. The meeting wasn't the alpha high up, booming down on us with his orders, a few public punishments to keep us scared, and a random introduction to a new Beta because… well that was never explained, but we all knew. Disagree with Carter and face the consequences, and in the case of his Betas, that consequence was being drained of your blood.

Here everyone stood around chatting. Had we not been aware of what this was, it would have seemed like just a social gathering, possibly a picnic because yeah—there was food.

"Our guests have arrived," Dylan announced, waving us over to him. "Let's do the introductions."

We walked over, whispers about Cujo still being a wolf and Kenon being so adorable the only noise surrounding us.

Once we got to Dylan's side, he introduced us one by one, the pack greeting us in unison each time with "Welcome, brother wolf". And then Dylan told him what little he knew about our situation. And what little it was. He needed to know more, to know the danger we brought and the reason for my protectiveness. He deserved better. They all did.

They opened themselves up to us, not one word of anything less heard or seen. And what did we bring them? Danger.

If they knew what was after us, they'd have reason to cast us all out into the cold and we wouldn't survive on our own. We were lucky to have survived the first time.

Had there been another way, I'd leave at dawn. We didn't have one. Not until Piers could shift. As a human he'd not make it an eighth of the distance we did as wolves. His body would be in worse shape than it already was. No. We needed to stay here and I needed to give Dylan the information he had to make the right decision.

It was time.

"Niko, as leader, would you like to say something?" Dylan handed over the floor to me and I froze. *As leader.* Only by default. This wasn't my calling, and in many ways I'd done a shit job, almost costing my brother his child.

"Ummm… thank you for letting us find respite." There. Respite was a good word. Fancy, even.

Of course, I started off with the world's longest ummm, but still.

"We promise to repay your kindness in any way that we can." Boom. That was better.

"You already have," Dylan said. "By giving us your trust."

If only that were true.

The next hour was spent meeting pack members individually. The chances of me retaining all of their names was nonexistent. But I did my best. Each and every one of them treated us with such kindness. That shouldn't shock me, but it did.

As they cleared the area, I caught the complete exhaustion on my brother's face out of the corner of my eye. "Let's get you back to the dorms." I wrapped my arm around him. "Thank you, Alpha."

"Would you like me to send Reeva your way?"

"No." My brother smiled at him. "I'm just tired. I'm not used to so many people."

"I hear that." Dylan let out a rich chuckle. I hadn't heard that from him before and I wanted to listen to it all afternoon.

The seven of us, the omegas and Kenon and I, went back to the dorms. Piers drank a big glass of water, as promised, and went straight to nap. Kenon did the same. Cujo never stepped foot inside, instead seeing us all there safe and then waiting for me to tell him it was fine for him to roam.

He didn't need my permission. I wasn't their Alpha. But I also kind of was. If only I were better at it and you know… an alpha.

I sat in the communal area trying to figure out everything. The more I thought about things, the more my mind went in circles, my feelings of self-doubt increasing with each rotation.

"Your wolf is restless." Lewis sat in the chair in front of me. "You should get some air. Piers is fine. Ralf and I will keep an eye on things while he sleeps and Seymour does the dad thing."

"If you stay out long enough I might even make pancakes for dinner." Ralf came up behind his brother. "The kind with bacon in the batter."

Those were the best.

"Fine. I'll leave." I stood up, my wolf loving the idea of getting out of the house and out of my head. "I'll be back in time for pancakes and if Piers needs anything…"

"I will run for Reeva in wolf form howling the entire way while Ralf helps him out here." They were good. Like they had a—

"You planned this." I rolled my eyes at them.

"Only about a minute ago," Lewis promised.

I took them up on their offer. They would give their lives to save a child, including Piers's baby. It was who they were.

My wolf was itching at me too much to get back to Dylan… for me to trust his ass. He'd taken Dylan's kindness as a sign he was our mate. My wolf seemed to have forgotten that we couldn't trust alphas. He didn't understand that we weren't staying here, and he really didn't understand that we were broken goods and Dylan deserved better.

So what that Dylan was hot and kind and scented like amber and honey. Those things changed nothing—not as far as mating was concerned.

I headed the opposite direction of the pack house, not wanting to run into Dylan and deal with the fight my wolf would give me there. If he had his way he would take his fur and sink his teeth into Dylan's wolf. What a mess that would be.

Or maybe he wouldn't and he was all bravado and talk... or rather, howl. He had his chance in the woods and decided to play instead. For a half second there I thought I'd messed up all things but being there with Dylan. Thank goodness my wolf hadn't pushed. I'd been so far back I'd never have been able to overpower him then.

I was stronger now, but not my full strength. Not by a long shot.

"You the new wolf?" an older man I didn't remember meeting, but who was scented like Northbay asked, startling me. "My grandson Dylan mentioned you were here. I missed the pack meeting because—it's best if I don't go to them."

I thought back to things Dylan had said about his family. His grandfather had been Alpha of the pack and his mate had passed. That was the sum total of what I knew about the man. It made sense he didn't go to meetings. There might be some who remembered him as Alpha and Dylan didn't need people clinging to good old days or bad old days or whatever they might be. He needed them in the here and now.

"I am." I bared my neck. "I am Niko."

"You can call me Gramps. Want some tea?" He pointed to a cabin, one far too large for one person. "That's my place and the water is already warming up. I even have cookies."

I could see so much of Dylan in him, or was it him in Dylan? Either way, they were both there in this old man and it made me smile and trust him a tiny bit.

"Who could say no to cookies?" I teased, because it sounded like the right thing to say. I actually didn't have a lot of experience with sweets.

"No one worth my time, that's for sure." The old man chuckled, his laughter holding the same rich quality Dylan's had earlier.

We went inside and sure enough, the kettle was whistling only seconds after we stepped inside.

He brewed a pot and handed me a cookie jar shaped like a wolf. "No sense plating a few out only to have to do it again," he explained, and we took our seats at the small table on a deck outside his kitchen door.

"I'd ask you to tell me everything, but I'm not one to waste my time." He reached in the cookie jar and pulled out a chocolate crinkle cookie the size of his hand. "So instead I have things to tell you."

"Okay." The silence grew between us enough for me to finally figure out that he was waiting for me to take a cookie. "Thanks."

I took a nibble. It was magnificent. The flavor burst from the morsel in my mouth and I bit back a moan. Sweets weren't allowed at Shadowpine. I hadn't had so much as a cookie, cake, or candy since leaving my birth pack, and even there, they were scarce. The cookies were little bits of heaven.

"I was mated. My mate hung the stars. When I lost Earl, it was like losing half of myself," the old man said. His gaze was unfocused as he stared off into space.

I set the cookie down. I'd thought he was going to give me a lecture on omega safety or something. I wasn't even sure what, but telling me about his dead mate was most definitely not on the short list.

"I don't regret one second of my life with him. Do you know what I do regret?"

"No, alpha."

"I regret all the time I missed with him because I was too stubborn to see that he was mine." He bit off a huge chunk of his cookie and then spoke with his mouth full. "I wish someone had told me to open my eyes back then." He took a long sip of his tea.

I froze as his words settled. They played over and over in my mind and I couldn't help but wonder if this man knew something I didn't. I was focused on surviving, keeping my pack safe and away from Shadowpine. My eyes were wide open to the cruelty of the world.

"Drink up. This is amazing tea. I made it myself

with rose hips from that bush out there." He pointed to the far right.

I tried it and he was right. It was amazing.

"Niko."

"Yes."

"Open your eyes."

Open my eyes. As if anything in life was that easy.

Chapter Nine

Dylan

"You think this next load of shingles will do the trick then?" Vaughn asked.

Hutch looked down at the pad of paper in front of him with the calculations on it. "It damn well better. I'm getting tired of this roofing bullshit." He tossed the pencil down and leaned back on the bench of the picnic table.

Our empty plates had all been pushed to the side a while ago to make space for the paperwork we'd accumulated for the re-roofing project. Each building in the pack had been reshingled in the last few months. We were on our last few buildings. Thank gods. Doing them all at once sounded like a great idea until we had to do them all at once.

"Once we're done, every house in the whole pack will have a new roof," Hutch said with pride.

Darren snorted. "Well, they better last long enough

to make it worth it. Hopefully we won't have to do this again for another twenty years." I was hoping for closer to thirty.

"As long as there are no storms." Hutch held up his hands, his index and middle fingers crossed in a wish for good luck.

I was only halfway paying attention. At the beginning of the discussion, Niko had emerged from the omega dorms, stealing my focus. My full attention was now on the lithe little omega that was currently playing a game of keep away with the young pups. It seemed that Niko was a wolf who could handle a soccer ball.

Pups in both human and wolf form played around his feet. They were nipping at his heels as he kicked the ball around and out of their reach. Niko wore a pair of shorts that were slightly too big on him and no shirt. The shorts hung low on his hips, exposing his hip bones. Sweat glistened on his skin, leaving trails of moisture down his chest. My mouth watered as I yearned for the taste of it.

Mate. Mine.

Vaughn turned around and followed my gaze. He grinned as he saw what it was that distracted me. A growl rumbled from my lips before I could stop it. My wolf hated the thought of another alpha's eyes on what he considered his.

"Everything okay, alpha?" Darren asked.

I snapped back to my Betas. "Yeah, fine. Everything's fine. So, shingles will be here next week?"

"No, they arrived yesterday," Hutch said. Had he said that already? He probably did. I needed to focus better.

"What's that?" I said absently, not listening to my own advice. But how could I when he was out there all distracting like? My eyes were glued to Niko. Now he was bouncing the ball on his knee while the pups watched in awe.

What was it Hutch had said again? I looked at him, but he just raised an eyebrow at me and I remembered. Shingle. Here.

"Oh, good. Even better." I turned my attention back to the omega. But he had moved from his spot. The pups had taken off with their school teacher Ilyssa, and Niko walked along the path toward my grandfather's house. I kept my eye on him as he walked up the steps and let himself inside. "Where's he going?" I muttered out loud.

"To visit your grandfather, clearly," Hutch said, barely keeping the chuckle from his voice.

A rumble erupted from my chest again, my wolf letting out his displeasure at being teased.

"Sorry, alpha," Hutch said.

I sighed. "Don't mention it." I ought to be the one apologizing. I wasn't a hardass alpha who couldn't handle teasing. This was different, though. My wolf was on edge and had been for days. I needed to snap out of it.

"Niko has visited your grandfather a few times since being here. I think the two just get along well," Darren said. "Reeva mentions that he's even got your grandfather taking his vitamins regularly. They've really hit it off."

I nodded. It wasn't difficult to get along with my grandfather. He was actually quite fun. What I wondered about was what they talked about. I didn't want Niko confiding in others. I wanted him to confide in me, tell me about his day. Tell me what brought him here, about his life in general. But I'd gotten nothing from him. Not since the day in the hot springs. He barely gave me a passing glance. And each day my wolf became more and more agitated about it. I found myself grumbling more, getting fidgety whenever anyone else was near him, anyone who wasn't me, which was pretty much anyone all the time since he wouldn't let me near him.

"Alpha, if I may…" Hutch began and I shot him a look. Fur erupted on my forearms and my claws extended. I took a deep breath to calm the change that appeared out of nowhere.

"Listen, don't give me that no nonsense alpha look."

Hutch pointed a finger at me. "I'm looking out for your best interest, which is part of my job as a Beta."

He was right. That was part of his job. I nodded and took a deep breath to steady myself and calm my wolf. "Go ahead."

"You clearly have an attraction to that omega," he pointed out.

"So?" I shrugged. I wouldn't deny it. I'd never lie to my Betas. "I'm not doing anything about it."

Mate.

"Maybe you should. Your wolf seems to be falling into a rut." Hutch raised his chin and stared down his nose at me.

I narrowed my eyes. "I am not."

"Are you sure?" He quirked his brow.

"Of course! It's impossible and unheard of." I scoffed. A rut. I'd only ever heard stories and had never known an alpha to actually go into rut simply because they were around an omega. It was ridiculous... a story to keep alphas from focusing on omegas that weren't theirs. It wasn't a thing. Not a real one.

Unless...

"Not if he's your fated mate." He confirmed what

my brain had been starting to realize.

"I'm not going into rut." I whisper-shouted the words, hating that it felt like a lie. My stance was clear, but I wasn't going to shout and alert the whole pack to the conversation. I didn't even want to be in this one.

Hutch held out a hand, ticking off fingers as he listed his reasoning. "You won't let anyone near him. You're being overly aggressive even with your closest friends, your Betas. You've growled at us several times during this meeting and all we did was look at Niko."

"It's nothing. Niko has just gotten under my skin." I waved a hand in the air, dismissing the idea even as it took root in my mind. A rut would explain a lot, though I hated to admit it.

"Sure. But we'll be keeping an eye on it. If it gets worse…"

I wanted to glare, but he was absolutely right. My wolf was off his game and did not like having any-one else near the omega but me. I wanted to tear apart anyone who looked at Niko. I really wanted to whisk him away to someplace private and be alone with him for the next month.

Fuck. It did sound like a rut.

"Meeting adjourned," I said and pushed myself to a

standing position. I walked quickly from the pavilion to my grandfather's house, the gravel crunching beneath my feet, stones flying as I pushed forward. No one stopped me or even said anything to me as I walked, which was unlike them. Clearly they could tell their alpha was on a mission. But what in the hell was that mission?

I ascended the stairs at my grandfather's house, the old wood creaking beneath my feet. His home was sturdy, but he didn't allow us to keep it in as good of shape as the others, simply because he didn't want us around all the time. Since his mate, my omega grandfather, had passed away, my alpha grandfather had become a bit of a recluse. It wasn't usual for a wolf to outlive their fated mate. Not by how long my grandfather had. It had been a decade since an illness took my omega grandfather's life.

Niko was just coming out the door as I went to open it. He gave me a look, his eyes narrowed. He was still shirtless and I willed myself not to ogle him. That sort of attention was not what he needed. Thankfully, my wolf and my brain obeyed and I kept my gaze locked on his.

"Alpha," he said, though he didn't show me the respect that other wolves did.

"Niko, how are you?" I said. My voice came out more gruff than I intended. The words were practically a growl.

"I'm fine, alpha. How are you?" He looked me up and down not in desire, but in questioning.

"I'm fine." Or fine-ish. Better now that he was there and I could scent him. "How are you?"

He cocked his head to the side, his lips pursed in the most adorable pout.

My words registered. "I mean—I'm fine. Fuck." That wasn't how this was supposed to go. I sounded like a lunatic, and I couldn't stop staring at him.

"Is that you, Dylan?" my grandfather's voice boomed from inside. "Close the door. You're letting the damned bugs in." There were no bugs, but he was right to ask me to shut the door. None of this was pack business.

Niko grinned. "I'll be back in a bit, Gramps," Niko shouted and then took off down the porch steps. *Gramps?* Since when did my grandfather become a Gramps?

My gaze lingered on the swell of his ass cheeks as he walked down the path to the pavilion. I could have just stayed at the pavilion and he would have come to me. Or maybe he was only going that direction because I wasn't there anymore. Damn, this omega was confusing.

"What did I say about the door?" my grandfather tsked.

I took a deep breath and stepped inside, closing the door behind me.

My grandfather sat in his recliner, staring out the window that faced the woods.

"Grandfather, how are you?"

"You don't usually visit me this time of day. Then again, you don't visit me that much anymore," he grumbled.

I chuckled. "I visit plenty often. If I visit anymore you'll grow tired of me. What was Niko doing here? I didn't realize the two of you are friends."

His gaze bore into me, one grey eyebrow raised. A slow smile spread across his face as he studied me. "You've been thinking about taking a mate at all, boy? It isn't good for an alpha of the pack to be without one. They bring balance, you know."

I groaned. "I know. I know. And it has crossed my mind." My wolf wouldn't let me entertain the idea of taking a mate of convenience now though, not with Niko in the picture. It was Niko or no one.

"Seems to me that an Alpha Omega should be strong, capable. So capable in fact that they could lead their own pack." He wasn't even attempting to be coy anymore.

I narrowed my eyes. "It's not like you to be cryptic, old man. Just say what you're thinking."

“That omega is your mate, Dylan. No doubt about it. He’s the one fate chose for you.” He sat up straight, looking every bit the Alpha he once was.

I shook my head. “He has a past. A history I know nothing about. I don't think the world has been kind to him.” And none of that was a good reason for him not to be my mate. None. Of. It. And yet I clung to it like a fool.

My grandfather winced. “No, it has not.” His shoulders sunk slightly. “Perhaps he needs someone who can show him how kind the world can be.”

My lips twitched and I thought. “I don't think there's any interest there. He avoids me.” And at the end of the day that was the real thing, wasn’t it. I was terrified to get my hopes up and wind up being wrong.

“You won't know until you ask.”

“What do you know about him?” I hedged, hoping for a clue, some insight that might help me to get closer to Niko.

My grandfather’s lips pressed firmly together. “I won't be telling you anything about what that boy has confided in me. That's knowledge for you to discover on your own, when he trusts you with it. And he will soon, if you do your part.”

“And what's that? What's there for me to do?”

"Grandson, if I have to explain that to you, then we've got a lot more work ahead of us."

Chapter Ten

Niko

I needed a task. Not like a *run this group of omegas* type of task, which contrary to what Northbay seemed to think was not an official thing or even one I wanted. No, I needed something to do that would keep my hands busy. A few times I almost offered to help with the roofing project, but every time I saw them working like the well-oiled machine that they were, I decided against it. I would be more trouble than I was a help and no one needed that.

Instead of roofing, I visited Gramps. I did things around the house for him and we chatted. He told me repeatedly not to feel obligated and I didn't. I just felt better helping out where I could. Keeping my hands busy kept my mind busy and the anxiety at bay.

So far I had done laundry, cleaned the bathrooms… so many bathrooms, most of which probably hadn't been used in months, and stripped some wallpaper. It wasn't overly skilled labor, but it made me feel like I was doing my part.

I'd shared more with Gramps than I had even shared with my brother. Not once, not for even a single second, did I feel judged by the man or worse—pitied. He just treated me as not an equal, but more like an adopted grandkid, and I loved that. I'd missed out on so much "normal" in my life and it was nice to have this.

My wolf was pacing and the new day had not yet officially begun. Everyone in the dorms was still asleep, as I should be. But I was itching to do something. I left a note by the front door and headed on out into the cool morning air.

I kept my skin, much to my wolf's chagrin.

It was gorgeous as the sun just peeked over the horizon. Soon enough the pack lands would come alive, but for now the peaceful silence was a balm, one that would allow me to think.

I spent the first hour wandering in the woods, careful not to leave the Northbay lands. It was one thing to accept their help, quite another to cause them problems by venturing into another's territory. Though, if I understood things correctly, they had a very friendly alliance with the bordering pack.

Making a list of things I wanted to do for Gramps

filled the time. It was mostly little things like fixing the runners on his one kitchen drawer to bigger things like refinishing his gorgeous hardwood floors. The list had two sections: one that required no money, just labor, and one that needed supplies the pack might or might not have and therefore might cost a bit.

I felt better having a plan, a plan to be productive. With Piers still not cleared to shift, we were going to be here awhile and I didn't feel right about us not giving back. I wouldn't push the others to do the same. Piers needed to heal, Seymour needed to regain his strength and take care of his young, Cujo was stuck in his fur, and the brothers were already doing things around the omega dorms on their own accord.

That all settled in my brain, my mind began to wander to dangerous territory—Dylan.

As much as I wanted to keep a distance from him, both emotionally and physically, I found it more and more difficult with each day. There was something about him that just called to me—called to my wolf.

It was more than him just being nice and hot, although he was most definitely both of those. No. There was something deeper there that sparked a connection between us, a connection I'd never experienced before. It terrified me.

Gramps hinted it was fated mates or some shit. And not really hinted as much as stated it mid-conversation and then moved on. At first it bugged me—his forwardness—then I took it as him being lonely and not wanting it to be the same for his grandson, but now? Now I was beginning to wonder.

Maybe he was right. My wolf sure thought so. And my dreams… they were all in on that plan.

Every night it would be Dylan and me together. Sometimes we'd be frolicking in the woods, just playing. Others he would be tracking me like prey only to end with him catching then knotting me right there on the forest floor. And then there were the dreams where we were both in our skin and usually only our skin.

And then inevitably I'd wake up hard, needy, and pissed it wasn't real—that our lives were not that simple.

But they weren't.

After all I'd been through with Carter and how he'd forced himself on me and my brother, being attracted to another alpha was shocking, but not unwelcome. I'd never thought I would feel that, but I'd wanted to.

Rustling leaves pulled me from my thoughts. I inhaled deeply. *Seymour.*

"What brings you out here?" I asked, and he

jumped out, shifting midway.

"The twins were playing with Kenon and my wolf was antsy, so I figured it was a good time to shift." He never met my eyes.

"Had nothing to do with you worrying about me at all?"

"You wore shoes." He was right. I had. Didn't think that was anything too alarming. If anything, it meant I had control over my wolf, something I wasn't always confident with lately.

"I did."

"Thought maybe you had—maybe there was a meeting or something." He bit his lip. "Like they were ready for us to move on or something and I thought you might want someone with you." That was a whole lot of what ifs he had mushed into one really bad scenario.

"Has anyone made you feel unwelcome?" It wasn't my experience but that didn't mean it wasn't his.

"No. Nothing like that. It's just—we are a liability to them, and I guess I worry they'll figure that out, but also I want to stay. I like it here. Everyone is so nice to the omegas… like they're just pack." He kicked a twig. "I want that for Kenon. I was thinking if we have to leave—he'd be safer here. They'd take good care of him." His voice cracked and my heart broke. To have to decide something like that—all of the *I want Dylan* crap in my head was nothing compared to what was going on in poor Seymour's.

I took a few steps closer to him. "You are the most amazing father." This time it was my voice that choked up. "Kenon is the luckiest pup in the world to have you."

"It wasn't fair to bring him into the world we live in." Tears started to flow from his eyes.

As if he had a say in the matter. He was bought and paid for…full stop. He was a victim in all of this. It wasn't as if he had gone out looking to start a family—it was forced upon him, literally, and given the circumstances… I couldn't go down that path or I'd be crying too. Instead, I pulled him in for a hug.

"The more time goes by the more I want us all to stay," I confessed. Could we? I had no idea, but the longing was still there, layering on the guilt I had for bringing us to their lands. They deserved better than us.

"The full moon is in two days." Seymour's tears ran down my chest. He didn't need to say why that mattered. I knew. All of us did.

The full moon was when Shadowpine liked to bring in new omegas and when they would cull the pack. The lucky ones were sold… the unlucky ones met their end. Or maybe it was the lucky ones who got to meet the goddess and leave this plane.

"Is it weird that just thinking about Shadowpine has me scenting them?" He sniffled.

I froze, standing up and taking in the scents of the air.

Crap. I did too. It was faint, but there.

A second scenting and it was gone.

"It's just our memories. They say scents are the strongest memory holders." Please let that be all it is, I thought. "Let's go back home and ask the others what they think about staying."

He agreed, and we walked back together, both of us pretending we weren't scenting the air with every breath, while doing exactly that.

We stepped into the omega dorms, the aroma of cooking bacon greeting us.

Kenon came running, his face beaming. He was already looking so much better than when we arrived and he was loving all of the good food, especially the bacon.

"Did you eat all the bacon, or did you save some for me?" Seymour bent down and picked him up. Kenon didn't answer with words, instead rubbing his cheek against his father's neck.

"There's bacon left, but there won't be if you don't get your butt in here," Lewis called from the doorway. "Your brother thinks being pregnant gives you bacon rights."

"It does!" My brother's exclamation came from the other room.

"Guess we better get in there." I chuckled.

It was as good a time as any to bring up our next move. We had time as Reeva had not cleared my brother, but it was better to decide sooner rather than later.

Cujo sat beside me, as the rest of us sat around the table. We were halfway through eating the bacon, eggs, and toast that Lewis and Ralf had made us when I bolstered the strength to bring it up. This was something we needed to decide together and then after we did, depending on our decision, we would need to discuss it with Dylan to see what to do next.

"We should probably talk about the elephant in the room." I grabbed another piece of toast to give me something to do. "Northbay has been very kind to us. Kinder than any pack we've been part of." I didn't need to elaborate more. None of us were here because we had a picture-perfect childhood. Our birth packs had sold us to Shadowpine. I wasn't sure of Cujo's history, but for the rest of us, that was fact.

"It is approaching the time when a decision needs to be made. Do we ask to stay on a more permanent basis, or do we continue to run?" I glanced around the table, no one looking shocked by my words. It had to have been on all of our minds.

"And if we run? Where are we going?" Lewis asked. "I mean really—we can't run forever. Maybe my brother and I can and Cujo too, but there's a child and a baby to consider. What is our end destination if we go?"

"I agree with my brother," Ralf said. "When we left our focus was on getting away and keeping us all alive. We need more than that if we are going to run again."

"But staying here—we're sitting ducks." Seymour handed Kenon a piece of bacon. "My son is a sitting duck."

"Seymour, I understand your fears better than anyone else here." My brother reached across the table and put his hand on the man's forearm. "Now more than ever. But it feels safe here—safer than any place I've ever been."

Silence filled the air at his words. I agreed with him. For the two of us, this was the safest place we'd been. But their stories weren't ours and they needed to decide for themselves. We were all going or all staying. Anything else made us weaker.

Finally, a few solid minutes later, Seymour admitted, "Agreed."

"We need to all agree." I looked down to Cujo, who gave a nod. Whenever I thought him more wolf than man, he would do something so completely human as that. "Cujo is in."

"I vote we stay," Lewis said.

"I'm with my brother in all things," Ralf instantly added on.

"I'm with you, Niko. You have never led me wrong in all my years. Where you go, I go. Where you stay, I stay." He settled his hands on his belly. "I mean we stay."

"That just leaves you and Kenon, Seymour." I took in a deep breath. I would accept their decision. "What is your vote?"

He looked to each of us and then back to me. "It feels safe here." He let out a sigh. "I don't love putting us on their shoulders but there is no place I'd rather raise Kenon."

And with his words it was decided. We would ask Dylan what the next steps were when the time was right. And maybe there weren't any steps to be taken. Maybe I'd miscalculated and we'd overstayed our welcome, but maybe… just maybe we'd found our home.

"If we ask to stay, we have to tell them about where we came from. Dylan has already asked. And if we tell them the truth, tell them about Shadowpine, we have to be prepared to leave if they tell us to."

My words were met with nods from each of them. We'd stay. Soon we'd ask to stay permanently. Likely I would be in charge of facilitating that conversation, and when asked, we'd tell Northbay the truth about where we came from and cross our fingers it wasn't a deal breaker.

Chapter Eleven

Dylan

As alpha, pack runs were my absolute favorite. It was a time for me to see my pack have fun and play together in a way that they didn't get to in their everyday life. Pack runs were a celebration of life, of the balance we had as both human and wolf. We celebrated our history and planned for our future.

Most official pack runs took place on the full moon, where everyone in the pack got together. Obviously, we were welcome to go on our own runs and shift whenever our wolf called to us throughout the month, but full moons were when we were at our strongest. It was when our wolf had the most power over our human side.

The gathering of the pack for a run as wolves helped to solidify the bond that we had, the shared purpose that brought us together. We were able to come together and enjoy each other's company. Each run as a group made us stronger.

The day of full moon runs were like our sacred days. We worked very little and socialized a lot. Everyone gathered for a large breakfast of eggs, bacon, sausage, and pancakes. Everyone pitched in to clean up afterward. Then, just before the run, we had a large meal, usually steaks. We were wolves, after all.

Full moon runs were also when we welcomed new members. If a mated pair so desired, it was also when we had our mating ceremonies. Alternatively, ceremonies for lost wolves, those that had left the pack and this plane, were held on new moons.

This particular night would be memorable for us. For me more than anyone else in the pack. This would be the first pack run with Niko's group. They wouldn't be officially welcomed as pack… We weren't there yet. But maybe they would see how welcome they were and what things could be like if they decided to stay.

If—I hated that little word. *If they decided to stay.* I didn't want there to be any question about it.

I'd already begun to think of Niko and his omegas as part of my pack, and having them run with us was a way to show them that. Each of his wolves had agreed to join us, except for Piers since he was still on modified bedrest. We'd invited him to eat with us, but he declined. I got it. Having to contain your wolf when they wanted out stung and doing so when everyone else was enjoying their fur would sting deeply.

They all sat at a table together, but with several members of my pack sprinkled throughout. They were integrated with us now. They smelled like pack more now—not completely, but enough to calm my wolf. No one seemed wary of them; instead my pack had done whatever they could to extend our hospitality. Niko and his group had gotten clean clothes, hot meals, and an abundance of cookies dropped off to them as a way of welcoming them to the pack.

I hoped that they would remain with us permanently. Having omegas around had already improved morale. Even Darren had mentioned the difference since the group had arrived. Not only that, but these omegas were eager to pitch in. Niko had done several small chores around my grandfather's home that I and my father hadn't gotten to yet. The twins, Lewis and Ralf, had helped with the garden several times. The omegas had brought balance to us and I was beginning to trust my wolf more and more each day when he urged me and called to Niko.

Mate.

I met Niko's eyes from across the pavilion. It was as if he heard my wolf's inner voice calling to him. *Mine. Mate.*

Inhaling deeply, I swore I could smell the jasmine scent that seemed so prominent on him. He smiled ever so slightly as we stared at one another. Joy and happiness shone in his eyes. His omegas surrounded him, smiles on their faces and light in their eyes.

There was a whole lot of hurt in the depths of Niko's eyes, though, beneath his tough exterior. Someday I hoped that Niko would share with me what it was that brought his pack to us and what he had gone through. I wanted to kiss those memories away and promise no harm would come to him again. I wanted him and I to make new, lasting memories together.

I wanted him. Full. Stop.

Once the meal was concluded, I stood on a bench. I didn't need to call attention to the wolves in the area, they instinctively looked to me as their alpha. Their wolves sensed mine.

"Pack, I'm so happy that we have gathered together on this strawberry moon. I know we are all itching to get out there and enjoy the warm summer night air. But I wanted to take a moment to extend a heartfelt welcome to our new friends. Niko, Seymour, Lewis, Ralf, Cujo, Kenon, and of course Piers and his babe, who are with us in spirit tonight." Knowing Darren was with him, keeping him safe, made his absence less stressful on my wolf, who was all about protecting them. They were important to Niko and Niko was my wolf's exclusive focus.

"As wolves we come together in solidarity to build a community of trust, mutual respect, and security and safety for all. It is my hope that we will one day soon welcome Niko and the others as pack members. For tonight, they run with us as friends, but soon it would be an honor for them to run with us as full-fledged members." I needed the new omegas to hear our welcome and for my pack to be clear on my intentions.

I held Niko's gaze as I spoke. Perhaps it was the breeze, but I couldn't help but notice a tear in his eye. Beside him sat Seymour, who held Kenon, who gleefully jumped and bounced in Seymour's arms. Cujo sat at their feet, still not trusting us enough to show us his human skin. Lewis and Ralf were close together. Those two were pretty much attached at the hip, but we had seen their walls break down as they began to trust us more.

Happiness showed on each of their faces and it was mirrored by my pack. Everyone was pleased to have these omegas with us. We just needed them to stay—it was a fine line of opening our arms and being too pushy and scaring them away.

I grinned as I looked out at my pack gathered under the pavilion. "So please, everyone, enjoy your run. Be safe out there."

With that, I hopped to the ground. By the time my feet touched the dirt I was in my wolf skin. My clothing shredded. I howled into the night air as my pack around me shred through their clothes and shifted to their wolf forms, their own howls answering my call. I winced at the waste of clothes coming from our "spontaneous" shift, but tonight called for it. It was a celebration.

I took off into the night, running through the forest, becoming one with the trees. The bright summer moon shone through trees, illuminating the trails we had cut. My Betas minus Darren flanked my sides to begin, but eventually as we ran, they went their own separate directions as we usually did when we were running.

My nose to the air, I sniffed the clearing and caught the unmistakable jasmine scent that I'd begun to associate with Niko. I slowed as I searched for him. He had to be close by. I was sure I had him spotted, but I knew my omega was a sly one. He was stalking me for a reason, and I was wary. I leapt to the side just as he was about to pounce on me. I turned in time to watch as he landed on the ground in front of me. He turned around quickly and his paws kicked up dirt and leaves.

He yipped a playful yip and we picked up our game of chase where we left off the last time we played in the woods together. As always, Niko was a formidable opponent, even while being playful.

He caught my neck several times, with his jaws clamping down enough to know I was caught but not enough to break the skin. He was deep in his wolf skin now, his human barely at the surface. I let my human side go as well.

Our wolves took over. We ran together, hunting down a rabbit. We worked in sync as if it was natural for us to hunt together. The way we maneuvered and communicated without words was like magic. The moon worked with us, illuminating the sky to allow us enough light to see, but enough darkness to keep our prey from seeing us. It was as if we received the blessing of the full moon.

With our prey clenched in our jaws, we took shelter in a cave not too far from the hot springs I had shown him before. Once our meal was finished, Niko licked his muzzle, his sharp canines glowing in the moonlight. It was late now and the howls from several of our pack mates echoed in the distance. I didn't generally stay out all night in my wolf form, but I was reluctant to leave and return to my empty home. With Niko by my side and my pack in high spirits, I felt no need to return to my human skin. I was content to stay and live in this moment for as long as I could. I didn't wish to worry about tomorrow or about Niko's past or our future.

Right now we just were, and that was all I wanted to be. The rut that had itched at my skin the past few days was alleviated with Niko by my side.

My wolf no longer hissed in my mind. *Mate. Mate.* There was no need. My mate was here, beside me where he belonged.

Chapter Twelve

Niko

I jumped over the log, his feet pounding on the ground behind me. I wasn't trying to lose him. Not really. This was a game. Our game.

I jumped onto a low branch and climbed the tree, just high enough I could turn things around and make him the prey.

Over the log he came, stopping long enough to scent where I was, but it was too late; I dropped from the tree, landing on him, wrestling him to the ground, my teeth grazing where I wanted him to wear my mark, his body shifting beneath me as I took my skin.

"My sexy wolf." His hand reached up and cupped my cheek sweetly. "I knew you were there."

"That either means you don't want me to know I got the better of you," I nipped his lower lip, "Or you want to feel my cock inside you."

His breath hitched. That was it. He wanted to be fucked

by his omega – fucked by me.

"Tell me, Dylan. Tell me what you want." Another nibble, my body grinding against his, our cocks both hard and ready. "Do you want me to fuck you here in the woods or do you want me to suck you down?" I nuzzled against his cheek, then whispered in his ear, "Or possibly both."

He groaned, his body shivering beneath me.

"Both it is." I bit his earlobe, my wolf extra bitey. "How did I get so lucky?" I started to kiss a path down his body, my own hot – so hot I was sweating.

No, not just sweating – a fever – I was burning up.

I rolled off of him to find myself standing in front of a fire – a huge fire back in –

I sat up, my body quaking, my senses on high alert, feeling the area around me to make sure this really was a dream and I was back in the omega dorms and not at Shadowpine.

Only, I wasn't in the dorms, I was in the woods. Dylan and I had spent the full moon night together and slept off the night's excitement in a cave.

The dreams I had were getting more and more vivid – my dream sex more and more adventurous since arriving to Northbay, but this was a new and very unwelcome addition to the mix.

Sweat was pouring down me and I pushed myself

to my feet. I was hot. So very hot.

And hard.

I padded outside to the cool night air. Water gurgled to my left and I followed the noise to a small stream. I splashed water on my face, giving myself a wash and allowing my hand to wander down to my cock. I just needed to get off and my heart would slow and my body could finally relax.

Or so I thought.

I didn't have a lot of experience with personal pleasure. Not since being with Shadowpine. But I had been a teenager once.

I leaned back against a rock and wrapped my hand around my cock. I gave it some long, hard tugs, thinking it would be enough given how hard I was, but it wasn't. Instead I had my wolf pounding at me: *Mate. Mate. Mate.* As he showed me pictures of Dylan.

Not helping. Not helping at all.

I thought back to the dream and the idea of having him in my mouth. It felt so good, almost too good—except it wasn't. Instead of reaching my climax it became the worst game of edging ever.

Giving up, I cleaned my hands, then drank some water, hoping it would cool me down.

Hot.

So hot.

Sweat was already forming on my skin.

Fuck. This wasn't the result of a bad dream or a good dream, for that matter. I was going into heat. I'd thought I was one of the lucky ones, one of the ones who never got one and never would. Heat meant danger for an omega—it was like a huge ass calling card to all the alphas.

A shiver ran through me, this time at the thought of when my friend Hank went into heat right before an omega sale. The Shadowpine bastards let everyone try him and—I couldn't go there.

I needed to leave.

I needed to be out of the way but not at the dorms. The Northbay pack were good people. They would never hurt us. But I didn't want a calling beacon on the omega dorms, not when my brother was still on restriction and all of us were still vulnerable.

I ran back to the cave where I'd left Dylan sleeping.

He was awake, sitting up. He stared at me, and his nostrils flared and his eyes widened with surprise.

"It wasn't a dream," he whispered.

Ours. My wolf was not helping.

"What wasn't a dream?" I asked cautiously, focusing on keeping my feet to the ground when my body wanted to race after him—to climb him like that tree in my dream, only sexier.

My dream. No. He couldn't mean… That was crazy.

"I—I've been rutting." He dropped his head. "And I had a dream. In my dream you came to me in heat… I woke up and you were gone."

Rutting? That was a thing? I thought it was an excuse alphas used to take advantage of omegas, but he wasn't trying to take advantage, he was sitting back staring at me, just waiting.

"I had a dream—it was good, but then bad and then I woke up and… I need a place to be safe, alpha." I fell to my knees and bared my neck, meaning to be all official and respectful like, and instead looking like I was offering to lick his thick shaft and then take it into my mouth until he hit the back of my throat.

Gods, that sounded perfect.

Ours.

"Safe?" His voice hitched.

"From the other alphas." I felt almost ashamed to say it. Like I didn't trust them. I did—but also I didn't. Nothing was making sense. "The only alpha I want is you and… is there a heat house here?" I hadn't seen one but that wasn't really the kind of thing one would point out to make new omegas comfortable, now was it?

"You can have the pack house," he said. "I can get you back to it safely." He didn't move, like the knowledge I'd just given him kept him in his seat.

"You don't…" I hated that I felt unease about him not replying that he wanted me too. "Never mind. I can—" I didn't know what; my brain was starting to get fuzzy again and I couldn't afford it to.

"I do want you, Niko. I have since the day you came into my life." My head snapped in his direction. "It's why I'm rutting—I think." He sat on his hands and I wasn't sure if it was so he didn't try to touch me or so I knew he wouldn't, but either way it gave me comfort.

And irked me.

I wanted him to touch me.

"Make sense." And probably why I was in heat when I never had been before. I never wanted anyone before—not like this. No. Not at all, and that was what made the whole thing doubly confusing… triply confusing… all the confusing.

"Let's get you to the house. You can make yourself at home. I'll tell the pack the place is off limits and I will crash with my grandfather for a few days. However long you need."

"Or…" I pushed myself to stand, my arousal no

mystery, my dick pointing right to Dylan… "Or maybe… make it stop." I pointed to my cock. "I tried to, you know, and I was even thinking of you, but it's like… I need you to do it." Gods, how embarrassing.

Dylan hesitated. His gaze was on my cock, but his hands were not. "I couldn't bear for you to wake up and regret what we did or to think I took advantage of you." Void from his explanation was any attempt to say he didn't want it.

A wave of heat, like that of a bonfire when the wind shifts and you are standing too close, slammed into me, my knees starting to collapse. I allowed them to, not able to fight it much longer, not wanting to.

"Please, Dylan. I've wanted—every night I dream of being with you and every morning I'm sad we could never be but maybe, for tonight, maybe we *can* be."

He stood up, came over, and scooped me into his arms. At first I thought he had decided to be all in, but then he ran with me in his arms. My body heat mixed with his until I was sure we were a thousand degrees. It wasn't until I heard a door shut that I realized where we were.

His home. He'd brought me home.

He was protecting me like I was his.

Ours.

"Let's get you inside." I snuggled up to him, hating that he wasn't inside me yet.

He brought me further into the house and set me down in the living room. "I will make sure you are safe." It was a vow, a vow that broke through the haze and landed someplace deep inside of me where it turned into a promise of something more—something he couldn't mean, but something I so desperately wanted.

He started to leave and my wolf tore through, blocking his way.

Not our finest moment. I forced a shift, my bones aching, my cock still hard. Stupid heat.

"Sorry. My wolf—he doesn't want you to go." As if that wasn't obvious.

"And you?" He stood there, a foot from me… twelve inches too far.

"I want you here, touching me, inside of me… and it's not the heat." Although the heat made it easier to say it or rather, more difficult to contain it.

"I couldn't live with myself if you regretted it." He took a step back. He was what alphas should be and not the ones I'd known.

"Every morning I wake up regretting it's only a dream," I confessed, not only to him, but to myself for the first time. "Please, Dylan. Please. I need you." In so many ways. But for tonight I would take this one.

I took a step closer and he matched my movement, his lips crashing into mine, our conversation over.

My hands started to explore his body as I explored his mouth, tasting him, feeling his passion through each motion. Everything felt right in the world except not. He was still too far away.

I pushed back, needing to see him clearly. His eyes were hooded, his lips swollen. Sexiest. Alpha. Ever.

"That's better." I raked my eyes up and down his body. "So much better."

He scooped me up again and jogged up the stairs as if I weighed but an ounce. "You deserve better than a fuck in the pack's common area," he explained.

I didn't care where we fucked, my mind already long past rational thought. I needed him in me… now.

He kicked open a door, the room scented like him, and he set me down on the bed. "Let me take care of you." He crawled on the bed and before I could miss his touch he had me in his mouth, my body bucking as he swallowed and sucked, licked and nibbled, my orgasm rushing through me so fast, my cum shooting into his mouth as the sexy alpha… my sexy alpha swallowed every last drop.

"I needed that." I panted as he came off me with a pop. "I needed that more than my last breath."

My head was clearer now. "Thank you."

"Omega mine, you don't need to thank me for doing what I have longed to do since we met." He kissed a path up my chest, my cock still hard because of the heat.

I let his term of endearment go, pretended it wasn't spoken even if it added more to that promise growing inside of me. "Quick, while your head is clear… tell me to go." His head was now inches from my own. He was giving me an out—making sure this was what I wanted.

"Please don't go," I said instead and he dipped his head to kiss me, this time sweetly, the taste of me on his lips the hottest thing I'd ever experienced.

"Thank gods." He kissed me hard. "Leaving would've been the hardest thing I've ever done."

"But you would have… without question."

"Without question." He kissed me again, and this time one kiss turned into two, then turned into endless kisses. My body started to heat up again, but this time the line between heat and natural desire blurred. It was him… Dylan… it was… *mine.*

Hands wandered, bodies grinded together, and when the need became too much, I asked for more and more he gave me, playing with my hole, praising how responsive I was, and then, sliding into me in one slow, perfect motion. My body opened for him like his cock was made to fill my hole.

"Home," he whispered, one tiny word that meant everything.

"Home," I mirrored back, pushing up, encouraging him to move and move he did. In and out, increasing with speed and pressure with each motion, precum dripping out of my cock.

I moaned in pleasure, reaching for my dick. "I've got you." His hand ensconced my cock, squeezing it at first, then jerking it slowly and firmly, not losing his rhythm for a second; it was too much, yet not enough.

Never before had my pleasure been anyone's concern. Carter, the only alpha I'd been with, and not by choice, never touched my cock. I was glad that Dylan was the only one who'd had his hands there.

"Come for me, omega mine." And there it was again, *omega mine,* and it hit every button, my climax barreling at me, my cum shooting out and covering his hand and my belly. Dylan bellowed out in ecstasy, his body stiffening up as he filled me with his cum and then his knot, our bodies connected together.

His knot.

It couldn't be.

Except it was.

"Home," I said as he collapsed on top of me, my consciousness fading rapidly.

"Mine," was the last word I heard as I fell into blissful sleep.

Not that we stayed asleep for long, my heat waking me up an hour later.

"Alpha?" I nudged him with my nose, me more wolf than human. My wolf was taking over and I allowed it, the haze of heat still enveloping me.

"Uh huh?" he said sleepily.

"We're going to need to do that again."

He grinned. "I was hoping you would say that. First maybe a shower would be in order."

I averted my gaze, ashamed that I'd allowed myself to soil the alpha's bed. It was like I was hit with a bucket of cold water, only it soured my mood and didn't actually alleviate the heat.

"Come with me, my omega. I'll run you a bath. It will be like the hot springs, only I'll have soap and I'll get to lather you up."

I peeked at him from my lowered gaze. "You want to clean me?"

He cupped my cheek, his thumb grazing my skin softly. "I want to care for you in whatever way you need, Niko. Always."

The sincerity in his words stopped my breath. So I followed him to the bathroom and watched as he filled the tub, pouring soap and scents in the water until it filled with bubbles. Then he and I sunk into the depth together. We explored each other's bodies and both my wolf and I truly were happy for the very first time.

Too bad it couldn't last.

Chapter Thirteen

Dylan

I woke up just in time to see the flick of a white tail leaving my bedroom where Niko and I had spent his heat together. It was chilly, the cold morning air hitting my skin like tiny icicles now that I didn't have the heat of my omega next to me. No wonder he had taken his fur.

The scent of Niko's heat still radiated through the room. But it was stale. The fever must have passed sometime during the night. The memories from the night hit me full force, sending arousal and unabashed joy pulsing through me. Mates. We were mates. Not just that, but fated. I'd found my fated mate at long last and he was an amazing, strong, fierce omega. I couldn't be more proud to call him mine.

There was no denying it, even if I were so inclined. I knotted not once but multiple times. He was my mate. Mine.

If the rest of our days together had even a fraction of the desire and passion that we had last night, then I would live to be a happy wolf. After the first time, there had been several more, just as intense as the first. Some joinings sweet, others filled with enough frenzy I was surprised we didn't break the bed. Each and every one of them perfect.

It seemed my elation was one-sided, based on the speediness in which my mate left my side. He'd felt my knot and he'd enjoyed it. I knew he knew what it meant, so why was he running from me? My heart rate kicked up a notch. I didn't like that he could potentially be trying to ignore what had happened between us. He couldn't escape or deny fate. He was mine, I was his.

My wolf growled and before I could even register what was happening, I had changed into my wolf form and ran after my mate. He was quick. But I was determined to keep him safe—the need pressing at me so hard I was no longer thinking things through, just tracking him.

I followed his trail, relieved that he seemed to be heading the long way through the woods toward the omega dorms. Likely he was avoiding walking directly from the alpha's house to the omega dorms to avoid gossip. I caught up to him just before we reached the pavilion, just out of sight from the rest of the pack. But still within hearing distance.

My wolf jumped in front of him to block his path; he stopped for a second, then dodged to the side to get around me. I knew his moves though, and I was quick to stop him. I shifted to my human form. I'd need words to get this straightened out.

"Niko, please talk to me." It came out as a plea and not a command. He didn't need an alpha commanding him.

He shifted as well. Thankfully, because I didn't know what else to do. Sure, I could use my Alpha voice to attempt to force him, but it felt wrong. He wouldn't appreciate it, even if it did work, and I would lose too much trust from him.

Shit. Following him might've done damage there too.

"Get out of my way, Dylan." It wasn't anger in his voice or fear. It was something else—something I just couldn't face.

There was a war inside me. My wolf pushed at me to keep Niko cornered, but that wasn't the right approach. I didn't wish to force him to do anything. Even if it was just talking. He'd had too much of that already in his life. "Promise me you'll talk to me and stop running?" My voice cracked, my emotions raw. I didn't have to pretend or be strong with Niko. He was my mate. I just needed to be me.

Niko's eyes fluttered closed and his body went still.

"Fine," he said with a sigh. He leaned against a tree and sunk to the ground to sit against the trunk.

I joined him, careful not to invade his space, but I wanted to be close to him. I missed his touch already. "Please don't run from me," I said.

He shot me a glare. "Why? Because we're mates now?" he said, the disgust clear in his voice, and I flinched. "Because you claimed my heat and you think I might be pregnant? You think you own me now and can tell me what to do?"

"No," I said, my voice pleading. "I want to help you." I ached to reach for him and pull him on to my lap. I vowed someday that I'd find a way to help him be more comfortable with my touch, with any affection. Today wasn't that day.

He rolled his eyes. "You think you're going to be some sort of savior alpha? That you can stop the pack that's coming after us?"

I kept my features neutral. I knew something was after the omegas. I just didn't know what it was and this was the first clue I was given. "No," I said. "I just want you, Niko. Whatever you can give."

"I have nothing to give," he shouted. "Nothing. Last night was a fluke. I am not your omega. I don't want to be your omega." A tear trickled down his cheek.

My breath caught in my throat and I nearly choked

from the pain—the pain he caused me with his rejection and the pain emanating off of him. My wolf whined and cowered. He couldn't have hurt me more if he had stabbed me with my own knife, and that hurt wasn't near as deep as what I felt coming from him. "Niko—"

"Drop it, Dylan. It was a mistake. My pack and I are leaving." There was no force in his words. He didn't want this. He was doing what he thought he had to. As bad as I suspected things had been for him—they were worse. There was no other explanation.

I went to reach for him, and thought better of it. This was not a conversation I could force on my omega. He clearly needed time.

My wolf whimpered at the thought of letting our mate walk away, but this situation would require patience and time. I couldn't force my omega to accept our mating. It wasn't in me. If he wanted to be let go, I'd have to respect that. Even if it killed me. I'd still make sure he was safe. Nothing could stop me from that.

I lifted my chin, more determined now than ever to find out more about my omega and to help him to trust me. I would do whatever it took to make him see that I was not like the alphas he'd met before. I was his alpha, always.

A wolf howled in the distance. An alarm cry.

Fear clouded Niko's features. "What's that?" he asked. He gripped my hand.

I took solace knowing that when fear struck him, his first instinct was to reach for me. "It's Hutch. He's found something that he needs me to know about. I've got to go."

To my surprise Niko moved closer to me, grabbing my bicep. His grip bit into my skin, much like how he had clawed at my back the night before.

"What is it?" he asked, clinging to me, his fear palpable.

And what did my stupid wolf do? He pranced around at the way Niko trusted me. My wolf needed to read the damn room.

"I don't know. Could be nothing. Usually is. There isn't much excitement around here." My gut said it wasn't nothing, but adding fuel to the fire that was his terror would help not at all.

Niko sucked in a breath. "Be careful."

I narrowed my eyes. "Please don't leave. I don't want to own you, to change you in any way. I just want to be with you," I said. "And I need to know you are safe."

My omega softened. He opened his mouth to say something, but another howl split the air. It was definitely not nothing.

Others within the pack were moving; though I couldn't see them, I could hear the bustle of activity.

"I have to go," I said. "I'll come to the dorms after I'm done. All right?" I wanted to bring him there… to make sure he was safe. But Hutch wasn't one to call me like this. He needed me there and now.

He nodded. "All right."

"We can talk then."

He nodded, his eyes clouded with worry.

"Take your fur and run straight there. Just in case." I kissed his cheek before turning away and shifting to my wolf form. Whatever it was that Hutch was indicating with his alarm had me racing in his direction.

My wolf hated walking away from my omega when he was clearly in pain, tearing himself apart because of what happened last night. If this were a regular mating we'd be secluded in our home for a day or so enjoying each other's bodies, but my omega was not a typical omega. He had trauma that I knew nothing about. I vowed to myself to do what I could to take care of him.

I hoped whatever Hutch was howling about could be dealt with quickly and was not something too serious. It was my responsibility to keep my pack safe, and I knew my omega understood that, but I still wanted to get back to him.

Hutch's howls filled the air, and I followed the sound to where he stood just on our territory line. It was the opposite side of where our territory butted up against Greycoast. This border met land owned by the human government, and we gave it a wide berth so we weren't seen by humans. The last thing we needed was to be hunted because some human saw us as a rogue pack of wild wolves encroaching on their homes or whatever excuse they made to take up arms or set traps.

Every so often, some of the young wolves dared each other to cross the line; perhaps that was what had happened last night. Please let it be that, I thought. Giving the young a stern talking to and a shit ton of chores was much better than many of the other possibilities running through my mind.

I shifted to my human form as I approached. Hutch did the same once he spotted me. Another of our pack members, a young wolf named Leah, was with him; she had been shielded by his wolf form.

"What is it?" I asked.

Hutch put a hand on Leah's shoulder. She shook with fear, her brown eyes wide. That wasn't like her. She was tough and strong. I had her on a short list to be a possible Beta when she was of age.

"An unknown wolf approached Leah last night

when she and the other teens were out on their run."

I clenched my jaw. I knew immediately this was what my omega feared. Whatever was after them had tracked them here. I felt it in my bones.

"What did he look like?" I asked.

Leah swallowed thickly. "He was big. The biggest wolf I'd ever seen. He was silver and white, and half of his ear was missing, like something had taken a bite out of it."

"Did he stay in wolf form the whole time?" I asked.

She nodded. "He followed us for a minute, but as soon as we spotted him, he took off. I brought Hutch here to where we spotted him." I wanted to snap at her, tell her she'd waited too long, but her fear had me holding back. She'd done the best she could. I would need to give all the teens who were with Leah and who saw the wolf a talking to about not coming forward right away. But not now. More important things needed to be done first. So despite my urge, I bit back a lecture on staying clear of this part of the territory; we could do that later. For now, fear would keep her and the other young pups away.

Vaughn and Darren approached in their wolf forms and took their skin once they were near.

"Vaughn, take Leah back to her home. Leah, let

Vaughn know who all was with you. We'll want to ask them what they saw."

"Thank you, Alpha," Leah said. "I'm sorry."

"I know."

She and Vaughn took their fur and trotted toward home.

"Do you think we have a lone wolf out there scoping the nearby packs out?" Darren asked.

Lone wolves were rare, but they existed. Many times they weren't a threat, just curious. They were no match for a full pack of wolves, so they didn't cause a lot of trouble, unless they were dumb, which might explain the missing chunk of ear. Chances were he wouldn't be breathing still if it was he against a pack, though. No. He didn't feel rogue.

I shook my head. "No. My instincts tell me this has something to do with our omegas. Whatever chased them away has finally caught up to them." I scanned the area around us, like I might see them out there, but the woods were silent. The scent of the wolf was thin; he wasn't nearby now, though I knew we weren't rid of him. I could feel it. He was here for my omega and I wasn't going to let him near Niko.

"Hutch, you had the most exposure to the scent. Follow it, but stay on our territory. I want to know where he went and what he might have seen. Let's meet later, we have a lot to discuss," I said. "Until we figure things out, we should only share things we know for sure."

They nodded at my order. We didn't need to have gossip scaring my pack and possibly scaring the omegas away. They were safer with us than on the run.

"Should we ask the omegas about who might be after them?" Darren asked.

I nodded. "Eventually. But not right now. I need to speak with Niko first."

My Betas were smart; they likely honed in on the change in my scent. They could guess what happened between Niko and I, but now wasn't the time to discuss it, especially with things not settled between the two of us. No it could and would wait.

"Let's get back. I want to talk with the pack and see if anyone else heard anything last night and to reassure them they are safe." Please let them be safe, I thought.

Hutch took off on the scent trail, while Darren and I headed toward home.

I steeled myself for a conversation with my omega. He had the answers to several of my questions, I just needed to prove to him he could trust me.

Chapter Fourteen

Niko

What had I been thinking?

What a foolish question. I knew exactly what I'd been thinking. Dylan was mine and not just because I wanted him, or enjoyed his company, or admired all he was accomplishing for his pack, or even because he knotted me—which whoa! That was a real thing. It would take me a while to wrap my head around that completely.

But no, he wasn't mine for any of those reasons. He was mine because he was. Fate deemed it so.

Mine.

My wolf had been right from that very first day when I assumed he was being protective of our family. Even then—just one whiff and my wolf saw Dylan for what he was. He was our mate.

Mine.

Which sounded too simplistic and like it made no sense, but at the same time it was what it was. He was mine because he was.

Dylan was mine and I was his.

Except—we couldn't be each other's.

Not really.

I came with too much baggage, as the human phrase went. Only I wasn't human and my baggage came with danger lurking around every corner and a group of omegas without a home. Shit. I came with a tractor trailer full of baggage.

Shadowpine would stop at nothing to get us back, and they'd take Northbay down in the process. I couldn't let any harm come to them simply because they were kind. It would kill me if something were to happen to them… if something happened to Dylan.

I wasn't sad Dylan was interrupted by his Betas. I hated that it had something to do with work, but it gave me time to break away and try and get my thoughts together. Being near him, his scent around me, his warmth caressing my skin—it didn't allow me to think clearly. When he came to find me I just wanted to jump into his arms and ask him to never let me go.

Instead I acted like an asshat.

Telling him I didn't want to be his omega was a lie. I did, but I didn't want to hurt him. I didn't want to bring danger to his doorstep. I was willing to give him up to save him. The split second when I feared Hutch was calling because of Shadowpine only reaffirmed that. If Dylan hadn't let me go home on his own, I'd be frozen in fear.

I went straight back to the omega dorms as he directed, hoping to be there before anyone woke up. I wasn't up for answering questions, and there would be questions. I climbed the steps and took my skin.

From the looks of things when I opened the door, I was at least an hour too late. The twins were sitting there drinking mugs of what I guessed were coffee, their hair barely damp and their bodies facing the door.

They'd been waiting for me. Of course they were.

"We were worried," Lewis said as he raked his eyes up and down my body. His worry looked more like judgement, which I deserved.

His brother elbowed him in the side.

"You mean we were worried before he came in scented like alpha and looking like he was used as a chew toy." Ralf chuckled, a forced one, no true amusement touching his tone.

I went straight to the mirror. They weren't wrong. I looked like a chew toy all right, but not one of the marks broke the skin. If they had, we'd be having a much different conversation.

"I'm going to shower," I grumbled, not wanting to have this conversation just yet… or ever. We had things to talk about for sure, but I preferred to leave my hickies out of the conversation.

I humphed off and straight to the shower.

The steam and hot water felt amazing. I was sore in the very best of ways and I couldn't even enjoy it. How selfish was I to be upset about not waking up in a soft bed with my mate's arms wrapped around me when so much was on the line? Last night was one thing. I'd been in heat. But now? Now I had other things to focus on besides the way he filled me so completely, the way he instinctively found all the right places to kiss and touch, the way he could kiss every worry from my body.

Pushing those thoughts as far down as I could, I reached for the shampoo. As much as I wanted to enjoy Dylan's scent on me, it was best to not have the distraction when I went back to Lewis and Ralf. There was no way they were going to let the subject matter drop. None.

I wanted to stay in the shower all day, let my worries flow off of me like the warm water. That wasn't how life worked—not my life, anyways. By the time I had the shampoo rinsed, everyone in the house except Kenon would know that I had been with the

Alpha and they'd want some explanations. No. It was best to hurry up and get the conversation over with, especially with Dylan promising to meet me back here.

Having those two things occurring simultaneously sounded like a piss poor plan.

I threw on some clothes, took a few deep breaths, and went downstairs where sure enough, they were sitting waiting for me.

Kenon was occupied with a set of plastic trucks that were left on the front porch for him. No one took credit for it, but I had a feeling it was Gramps. He was really invested in us staying for some reason. *Because he knew what I needed a freaking knot to tell me.*

"Yes, I was with Dylan but it's because I went into heat."

Seymour gasped, and I felt beyond guilty for not prefacing my statement with "I went to Dylan" because Seymour knew how heats for unmated omegas could turn out.

"Let me start over." I walked around and sat on the couch. "Dylan and I—we are attracted to each other." That wasn't even close to better.

They just stared at me, waiting for me to continue, so I did. "And I've been having… Let's just say I wanted it. He isn't like *them*." I didn't need to say who *them* was. We'd all lived that horror in one respect or another.

"I want to believe you." Piers reached out for my hand. "I do, but to take advant—" he choked up.

"He very much did not. He—I—he knotted." I hadn't wanted to share that much, but there was no way I could describe heat sex and have it not lead them to the worst conclusion without it. Besides. They deserved to know. Keeping things from each other was not the way to survive.

Cujo walked over and nudged my hand with his nose. "What?" His eyes went straight to where a mating mark would go if we had gone that far. "Oh Cujo, that's not why I'm not marked. I… I'm the one who keeps putting on the brakes. Dylan… this entire pack deserves better than what we bring to the table."

"Fuck that." Seymour scowled. "We're all too good for where we came from and we'd be an asset to any pack. Don't let all the whispers that filled our lives take up root. Don't. It will only get us right back where we came from. Maybe not with the Shadowpine but somewhere just as bad." I refused to think there was anything as bad. "I want to stay."

"Same," the twins said in unison.

I turned my head toward Piers, who spoke. "I want to stay too, but Dylan needs to know. He needs to know everything and that sucks and it might mean they ask us to leave but not telling them… that only tells them we are selfish jerks." Once again, my little brother was the smart one.

I should've told Dylan earlier.

"They can't protect us if they don't know what they are protecting us from," Seymour added.

"But if they know then they are complacent. Shadowpine can seek retribution." Lewis stood up. "It's not as easy as just telling them. Once they know, they cannot un-know." He started to pace the way he did when his nerves got to be too much. It was a very wolf thing and I had a feeling it was his way of controlling his wolf.

"But if they don't know they can't be prepared," Ralf said. His brother was right too.

There was no easy answer. Nothing about this was black and white. Nothing.

"The Shadowpine won't believe them if they say they didn't know." Seymour rubbed his knee. "They don't care. They will do and believe what they want to achieve their end. We need to not factor that into the equation."

We went round and round trying to figure out what to do. The only thing we did decide on for sure was that at the end of the day, our desire was to stay here and become pack. I needed to talk to Dylan.

This wasn't our decision to make, it was his, and only after he had all of the information.

"I will talk to him. If Dylan wants us to leave after learning everything, we leave." I wanted to believe that would never happen. I was his fated mate, surely he'd let us stay. But I had seen too many cruelties in the world to know for sure that I wouldn't be turned away. The twins and Piers nodded in agreement. Seymour shook his head. "You would stay here unwanted?"

"I will not agree to give Kenon a life on the run. I won't. If they want us to leave, I will beg for asylum for my son. Once they take him as pack, he will scent as pack. He'll be safe. He already looks different than when we left." And he did. He'd filled out from the nutritious food and had already grown an inch taller.

"I... okay." It would break Seymour's heart and I would do everything I could to prevent that outcome, but I understood.

"I wasn't asking your permission," he snapped and got up off his spot and over to where his son was playing.

"I... I know."

The door opened and in came Ilyssa. My heart began to thump in my chest. No one came in here unannounced. Not even Reeva when they had an appointment with Piers. No one. And from the look on Ilyssa's face, she had a reason to avoid wasting time by knocking.

"The Alpha has sounded an alarm." Her voice was calm, her eyes all wolf. She was faking her ease and not well. "That means you need to stay in here until we let you know it's safe to venture out. The Betas are on patrol and you'll be safe."

"What kind of alarm?" Nothing in the air felt like a storm brewing, but I longed to hear her say there was a tornado coming and not something else.

"Nothing to worry about. Someone crossed into our territory yesterday, someone not pack, and we are shoring up the borders is all." That was not nothing to worry about. Not even close.

"What did they look like?" *Please don't be Shadowpine. Please don't be Shadowpine.*

"I don't know. There's no reason to think they're a threat. They chased some younger wolves and if they had wanted to do them harm, it would've been easy enough. They probably got turned around after hunting in the state park." I'd put money on it not being that. The pack territory was marked clearly. Sure, a human might cross over by mistake. But a wolf? Never.

"No one was hurt or even close. This is just a precaution." She kept taking a half step back, as if she needed to be out of here to warn others. It was unfair for me to interrogate her this way.

"We will stay put," Piers promised.

She took his word at face value and went to what I assumed was the next place she needed to sound the warning.

"They found us." Seymour looked up at me, Kenon in his arms. "They found us."

He was right. That was the only explanation. They were looking to see if we were here. They weren't going to decimate every wolf they crossed looking for us, but once they found us, they would take no prisoners. No. That wasn't true. They would take prisoners… each and every omega they thought they could use. The alphas…

I shook just thinking about it.

"Maybe or maybe not," I lied. "I'll go find Dylan. If it is them, he needs to be made aware of everything. Cujo—protect my brother." Piers may have told her we would stay put, but I made no such promise. If we brought danger to their doorstep they were owed an explanation of what that danger was.

Cujo padded over and bared his neck.

"We will keep Kenon safe," the twins vowed. I

hated to leave them so vulnerable, nothing more than sitting ducks, but I had no choice.

I stripped and took my fur. I had a better chance of finding him that way.

The scents—so many scents. It wasn't just the Betas patrolling. He had all the alphas out, making it harder for me to pick up on his most recent scent.

Amber and honey.

Mate. Go.

I sunk back and allowed my wolf to take over. He would find him better than I could. I had too many things flitting around in my brain. I had brought all of this to his pack. If I had only been more open, he'd be prepared for what was about to happen. Or maybe prepared wasn't the right word. No one could be prepared for the kind of cruelty the Shadowpine embraced.

But he would at least be aware of what was coming.

If anything happened to him or anyone else in this pack because I didn't tell him soon enough—didn't allow him to make the choice—I'd never forgive myself.

Chapter Fifteen

Dylan

My wolf paced within me, snarling with anger at the fact that my territory had been breached. As alpha, it was my responsibility to keep my pack safe and secure, and having our territory infiltrated by some unknown wolf likely intent on harming my pack made my blood boil. I protected my pack above all else. Having a mate, even if he didn't yet wear my mark, only intensified the feeling.

The trespassing didn't come from the Greycoast side. And even if it had, I knew they meant us no harm. But having these strange wolves on my territory had my wolf on edge. It was as if he knew something that I did not.

As soon as we were close to the pack house, I shifted back to my human form. My wolf was too hyped up to be around pack like this. They'd know something was wrong and I didn't wish to cause any panic. Sounding the alarm and having my pack shelter-in-place had been a hard call, but it was necessary. It was an odd feeling for me to not have control over the wolf inside of me. As alpha, I needed to keep a cool head. I needed to calm down for my conversation with Niko. He didn't need to see me going all alpha.

"Dylan!" My omega, Niko, ran to my side throwing his arms around my neck.

I held him against me and he shook, and the fear that radiated from him nearly choked me. Having him close and safe in my arms calmed my wolf, but the fear fueled the anger my wolf had at the events of this morning.

Niko's behavior was a night and day difference from the reaction I had from him just an hour ago.

"What is it?" I said. "Is everything all right?" I wrapped both my arms around him and molded him against me.

"Yes." He sniffled and he stilled. He stumbled back, the blood drained from his face.

"Niko? Are you alright?" I reached for him, but he back-pedaled, moving further from me.

"I have to leave," he said. "I have to take my—"

I grasped his hand and pulled him down to the ground with me, gathering him into my lap so I could envelope him in my embrace. It was what I had wanted to do this morning, before being called away. I wouldn't let the opportunity pass me by again.

"Take deep breaths, Niko. What's going on?"

His face contorted until I wasn't sure if he was going to cry or snarl. Tears pooled in his eyes, but he blinked them away. He struggled against my hold. "I can't! I can't tell you! I thought I could, but I can't. It's dangerous. Let me go!"

I kept my grip on him firm, but gentle. "Niko, please, mate. Trust me. Trust my pack. We can help you."

Sobs shook his shoulders until he took a deep breath, fighting down all his emotions. "It's Shadowpine. They're here for me. I brought them here. They won't rest until they get us back."

My wolf growled and my claws extended. I took deep breaths to keep the change from overtaking me. "Who is here for you? What are you talking about, mate? I need more information."

Niko sighed and buried his head in my chest. "We escaped," he said. "Months ago. And we've been on the run since. I thought maybe we lost them—bought some time. We were never going to stay in one spot for so long, but I couldn't risk Piers's baby." He looked down, his voice almost a whisper. "I hoped they would just leave us alone—I knew better but I wanted this to be home. But they will never leave us alone. Never."

"Who? Who won't leave you alone?" My focus turned from getting my mate to trust me to ridding the world of whatever threat was out there that was after my omega. My mate. My wolf wouldn't rest until this Shadowpine pack was eradicated.

"Can we— this might be easier if we talked at home," he said. His eyes were filled with pain and fear. There was a storm beneath their depths that twisted my stomach. What had my mate been through? What lurked in the shadows and scared my fierce omega who stood up to alphas and protected his omegas?

I nodded. "All right. Let's go." I stood, pulling him with me. I scooped him into my arms and cradled him against me. Here he was safe and his wolf settled. If he were a cat, he'd purr.

"You don't have to carry me," he said, but there was hesitancy there. He didn't want me to put him down any more than I wanted to put him down, and snuggled in a bit closer.

"I want to. No way am I letting you go, omega mine. You're safe with me, your wolf knows it."

People stared as I carried him down the paths to my house. Of course my home was centrally located and within view of everyone. There were no secrets when you were Alpha.

We received a lot of shocked expressions and a few knowing smiles from the few members of the pack that were out and about following protocol. Reeva winked at me as we passed.

I ignored them all. Soon they'd know about me taking Niko as my mate. Already, our scents mingled some and anyone close to us would know we were fated, that he was mine and I was his. Once we marked each other they wouldn't even need to be close to us, our scents almost identical.

Together we'd lead the pack.

Protect. Yes. After the threat was taken down.

Inside the house, I settled him on the couch and handed him a glass of water. Thankfully, someone had dropped off leftovers from last night's feast, including some cookies. I gave him one of the large chocolate chip cookies. He broke a piece off and nibbled on it, but didn't quite eat. After we talked, I would make sure to get a full meal into him.

"Start at the beginning," I said. "Whatever you want to tell me, I want to hear, okay?"

He leaned back into the couch. "I barely know where to start." He scrubbed a hand down his face.

I settled next to him and squeezed his hand. "Take your time."

He relaxed and let out a slow breath. The anxiety melted from him the longer I kept touching him.

'"Piers and I came from a small pack," he began. "It was a quarter of the size of yours. We didn't even own the territory we lived on. I think humans did. It was protected land, though." That wasn't unusual in and of itself. It wasn't ideal but not uncommon.

"We spent most of our time in our wolf form there, hardly any time as humans. It was very different than how most packs live." Antiquated was what it was. Shifter packs were like that many many generations ago, but now it was almost unheard of. "We had more omega wolves than we did alphas in my generation. So, when the opportunity presented itself to make some money, my pack sold Piers and me to the Shadowpine pack."

"Sold you?" I said slowly, my gut wrenching. Please let me have heard him wrong, I thought.

Niko nodded. "It was awful from day one. Piers and I were separated for several months in holding and then again after Shadowpine bought us. We thought things would be better—that someone would buy us to do work or something. But it wasn't. It was worse. They—we were kept in cages when we first got to Shadowpine." A tear streamed from the corner of his eye.

"Shadowpine isn't so much a pack, not in the truest sense. It's just a group of alphas who run drugs over the border between countries for humans. They make a lot of money doing it." I pushed my wolf down. He wanted to take over and hunt down this pack without so much as a direction to go by. He didn't care. He needed to do something. Anything to protect our mate.

"They're good at it because we're wolves and can do things that the human drug runners can't. The humans don't know what they are." If they did it would be a real easy fix. There were laws about exposing your true self to humans that weren't pack and we'd be able to hold them accountable. That was the one rule that could not be broken… ever.

In the past when shifters were found by humans they were experimented on and eventually killed by them. Or at least that was the story we were told growing up. There was a shifter council that usually took care of any transgressions against our sacred rules. Apparently Shadowpine had snuck through the cracks somehow, managing to break the human rules without getting caught.

"The alphas talk about how dumb the humans are all the time, that the human police can't ever catch them."

He went silent and I waited to see if he had more to add. When the silence grew the span of a couple minutes, I asked. "What did they want you and Piers and the other omegas for?" I clenched my fist as I awaited his answers. I could guess, but I wanted to hear it from his lips. He'd already hinted it wasn't work, leaving something so vile I was pretty sure I didn't want the answer even if I needed it.

Niko met my gaze and I knew the worst was yet to come.

"They use omegas for breeding purposes and their own disgusting entertainment." His voice got softer with each word as if he were ashamed. I hated seeing him like this and hated the reason he was like this even more. "Sometimes they sell omegas to other packs like them, or to lone wolves for… whatever. Once an omega is sold, they don't come back. We never see them again."

A muscle ticced in my jaw and I feared I'd crack a tooth with how hard my jaw clenched.

"Carter was my alpha."

I growled.

Niko's lips twitched into a grin, before he frowned again. "He was never actually mine. I was never his. You are my alpha, Dylan. I know that now. Piers and I were assigned to Carter. He's the father of Piers's baby. He… He was never able to get me pregnant. I don't know why." Niko averted his gaze, and continued. "When the midwife mentioned they thought that Piers was about to have an omega child because he didn't gain enough weight… I overheard Carter say that the child and Piers would be killed because an omega breeder was useless and no one wants to buy someone who had a pup. I had to get him away."

Niko took in a huge breath and let it out slowly and then another. I didn't push. What he was saying had to be incredibly hard to get out. But my omega, my strong omega, he was doing so without so much as a sob.

I wanted to sob and destroy things and hug him close and let him know I'd never let him go back there and would always keep him safe. But that wasn't what he needed from me right now. He needed to get it all out and as Alpha of the pack, I needed to hear it.

"He wasn't the only one things were getting dire for. The cruelty Seymour faced… we had to get out—all of us. There was no time left." He closed his eyes. "I had only a half of a plan that day, but it grew and grew. I knew it had to be perfect. If it wasn't we'd all end up dead."

He looked up at me. "I tried to escape before. The scar on my brother's neck—it's because I failed. He will forever wear the sign of my failure."

"You didn't fail him, omega mine. You got them all the way here—to me—to us—and we will keep you safe." It was a vow. I only got a glimpse of what they'd been through. What strong, brave omegas they were.

"I believe you." His words had my wolf prancing at his praise.

"This is awful, but when we got away, for a minute...I hoped they would just find other omegas." This time he did sob from the guilt he was carrying around for trying to survive. "I mean, that sounds awful because I would never wish that life on anyone, but I was hoping that they would at least leave us alone, but apparently they aren't."

"Whose scent did you catch out there? Was it Carter's?" My wolf started to gnaw, ready to come out. He made no secret of the fact he wanted it to be Carter so he could bleed him dry.

Niko nodded. "On my way here. It was faint, but I'll never forget it. It haunts me." He looked up at me with his tear-filled eyes. "Before the full moon, when I was with Seymour in the woods, we were talking about Shadowpine, and for a split second I thought I scented them, but we were talking about such bad memories and memories connect so deeply with smell—I didn't know. I'd have told you. I swear it."

I pulled him close and rubbed against him. My wolf was ready to scent mark him in any way that we could. We'd rub ourself against him until we couldn't tell our own scent from his. "Of course, you didn't. You're strong and brave and protective, but right now, it's okay to be the one protected. I won't let them get you—any of you. We'll take care of them and keep you safe."

"If you want us to leave, we will. If we leave now, Shadowpine will follow, and your pack will be safe. But please. Keep Kenon. He's safe here, he won't be recognizable to—"

A growl tore from my chest, silencing Niko. "You will all stay. You are all pack now. You are Northbay. Do you understand me?"

Niko nodded.

"You are mine. I am yours. This is your pack now. We will not abandon you ever," I vowed. I hated that he didn't trust us, but in time that trust would grow.

"They're dangerous," Niko said.

"So am I," I argued. Eventually, I'd need more details about where Shadowpine was, who they all were, and whatever else Niko and his omegas could tell me, but for now Niko had enough talking.

"Seriously. Dylan, you don't know what you're up against. I—" Niko hiccuped a sob. "I watched them murder Kenon's uncle, Seymour's brother, right in front of Kenon. He'd tried to stop one of the alphas from hitting Kenon, so they made an example out of him. Kenon hasn't spoken since."

My heart ached for the sweet child who'd just started coming out of his shell. He still didn't speak that I'd heard, but he was slowly coming around. We hadn't yet scratched the surface of the healing needed to repair the horrors he'd seen.

I kissed Niko's head. "I happen to know a group of people who could take down a dark healer; some drug runners are no match for me and the friends I have. No one will get to you. They will have to get through me first and that Will. Not. Happen."

Chapter Sixteen

Niko

I'd spent so much time being strong that when I finally let go, sobbing in my alpha's arms, it just kept coming. He held me close, rocking me, promising me he would take care of me. Whispering words that I'd never heard before. He cared for me, he'd help me. He'd keep me safe, keep my pack safe.

No one had ever promised to take care of me before. Not my fathers, not my pack, not my owners… no one, and here he offered so completely. Protection for not only me, but my brother as well.

A knock at the door had me freezing, then climbing off his lap, my heart beginning to race.

He got up and walked over to the door, his stance strong, all Alpha capital A.

"Darren, what's the word?" he started to say before the door was fully open. "Did you find them?"

"No, Alpha. The newest scent is at least twelve hours old. How should we proceed?" Dylan stood out of the way and Darren stepped inside.

"Let's keep patrolling and I'll give the Greycoast Alpha a call." They kept talking for a few minutes, but my head was too fuzzy from all the crying to pay much attention after they said the scent was a half day old. That was the important part. They weren't here. At least not now.

Best case scenario they thought we weren't here either. Worst case scenario we had time to plan.

"Mate," Dylan's hand caressed my cheek, "I need to call the neighboring pack's Alpha, Byrom, to let him know to be on the lookout."

I pushed to get up. "I can go."

"No." He tapped the tip of my nose, playfully, sweetly. "I want you to come with me to my office. I'm not ready to let you out of my sight just yet."

He held his hand out for me and I took it as we went to his office and called his friend.

How different that was from Shadowpine or even my birth pack. Alphas were to be feared and honored. They didn't have friends. But Dylan did. You could hear it in the tone of his voice and the way he asked about the pack's young and the alpha's mate. Dylan was the antithesis of every other Alpha I'd met, not that there had been many. But still.

"You are an Alpha of worth," I said as he hung up the phone.

"And you are an omega of worth." He walked around his desk and placed a sweet kiss on my cheek. "There's nothing more to be done here. Let's get the forest off of you."

I agreed, assuming he was going to set a shower for me. I was so wrong and it brought back memories of my first bath, the one he drew for me.

"Did I tell you my grandfather had this put in?" He turned on the faucet of the huge clawfoot tub; in the midst of my heat the night before I hadn't noticed the tub's build at all. "Said no pack house should be without a tub big enough to soak your worries away."

"I can see Gramps saying that." The steam started to billow over the lip of the bath.

"You're the only one who calls him that," Dylan noted, reaching for a bottle of bubble bath.

"I don't have to." Stepping on toes was the last thing I wanted to be doing.

"Nope." He popped the lid, lavender and amber tones radiating from it. "I like it. It means he likes you." He poured it in, the scent deepening as it hit the hot water.

"I like him too. He—don't be mad—but I kind of

told him some things about my past before—before you." I looked down, embarrassed by what I'd just admitted. It wasn't like my wolf hadn't already declared the man ours at the time—I'd just been too stubborn to believe it and there was something about Gramps that made it easy to share. Not the dark stuff—I wasn't ready to share details about that with anyone. But he'd known a bit more than Dylan had and it weighed on me.

"He's like that. Easy to talk to." He turned off the faucets. "I think the temperature is good. What do you think?"

I reached in and it was heavenly. "Perfect."

He helped me in and I sunk back, allowing the water and the scents to do their job and relax my muscles.

"Thank you. I needed this."

"That's what mates do. They take care of each other… give each other what they need." He grabbed a washcloth and dunked it in the hot water. "And right now you need a hot soak in a deep tub."

He had me lean forward and began to gently rub my back with the cloth.

"What if I can't give you what you need?" I blurted out, my attempt to find a better topic an epic fail.

"You are you." He kissed the top of my head. "And

fate sent you to me, meaning you are exactly what I need."

"Maybe I was when fate sent me but—remember what I told you about why Piers was pregnant instead of me."

He froze for a split second and then sat back on his heels, his eyes glued to mine. "It is one of the many reasons I will bleed Carter dry."

"No—not—I mean—what if I can't have kids? What if the reason I never got pregnant was because I can't? Carter—he did things to me—what if I'm broken?" Great. And just like that I was back to crying again.

Only this time I wasn't crying over what had happened to me or my crew—this time I was crying over what may have been stolen from Dylan's future.

"My heat was over so fast and what… what if I can't…"

Dylan stood long enough to get his clothes off. "May I join you?"

I slid forward. "Of course you can." He had me so confused as he nestled in behind me and settled my back to his front.

"That's better. My wolf—he needed to feel you were okay," he explained, his arms coming around me.

"You are my mate. You are everything I need. If we have children—great. If not—then we don't." He kissed my shoulder. "I need you exactly as you are."

"But you need an heir." Which was Carter's entire reason for—for so much of his cruelty to me. "I might not be able to give you that."

"There is no part of me that cares about power. None. Gramps says that's why I will fill his shoes the way they were meant to be filled—whatever that means. But if I don't have a child then my brother's child will be the heir, or one of my Betas. Hell, Piers's child could be Alpha someday."

"You really would be fine with it." I'd grown up being taught the entire purpose of my existence was to make babies—then I was sold to Shadowpine, where the entire purpose of my existence was to make babies, and when I failed, my brother paid the price. "How did I get so lucky?"

"That's my question. I am not sure how I got so lucky to have you, and the answer is Fate. She kind of knocked it out of the park. Now let's lay back and enjoy the hot water while it lasts."

We relaxed in the water, his arms wrapped around me. He told me stories of his childhood and about his brother, all the things that had nothing to do with the situation we were in now. We talked about favorite foods and colors and how we liked our coffee—normal get to know you things. It was exactly what I needed. It was like a time out of all the chaos that was my life and when the water started to chill, I wasn't ready for it to be over.

"Let's get you dried off and warm." Dylan slid out from behind me and climbed out of the tub. "Here." He held his hand out for me and helped me out, not like I was fragile. No. More like I was precious. He grabbed a towel and dried me off from head to toe and then dried himself.

"I should be saying you don't have to," I whispered, "but I like it. I like being taken care of like this." I never had in any memories. "Thank you."

I leaned in and gave him a sweet kiss. It didn't stay sweet long, our bodies pressed together, our scents enveloping us, our kiss deepening. It wasn't like our heat joining. There was no frenzy. This was more.

"Take me to bed, alpha mine," I pleaded as our lips broke for us to catch our breaths. "I need to be closer to you."

"There's nothing I want more." He gathered me in his arms and carried me the short distance to his bed, setting me on it gently and lying beside me.

"How am I… how?" He cupped my cheek, wonder in his eyes. "Promise me you'll never leave." His voice cracked slightly, raw with emotion.

"I don't think I ever could." Even if it were the right thing. Leaving him would break me in a way I'd never be able to recover from. Ever. I spent my life thinking my wolf was my other half.

I'd been wrong.

It was Dylan this entire time.

I rolled onto him, peppering his face with kisses, wanting, needing to explore his body—to memorize it—to taste it all. I worked my way down his neck, paying extra attention to the spot where I longed to mark him, enjoying the way he wiggled beneath me, his wolf rising close to the surface, begging for more.

And there would be more. Just not today. Today was about our human side.

I continued my path until I reached his nipples, kissing and sucking one as I teased the other with my fingers, switching sides, enjoying how I could make him squirm with arousal. But I wasn't done yet. His rock hard cock, pressed against my chest, his precum moistening my skin—that was my goal.

I needed to taste him—swallow him—watch him come undone underneath my tongue.

Looking up at him, I announced my plan. "I can't wait to feel you in my mouth."

He swallowed deep, his wolf shining in his eyes. I slid down, kissing, licking, nibbling the entire trip. My tongue darted out, swiping away the precum.

"Delicious," I praised as I wrapped my mouth around his tip, circling it with my tongue, enjoying the moan of pleasure coming from my alpha.

Mine.

Mine.

Circling, licking, sucking, swallowing, I worshiped his cock the way it needed to be worshipped, loving every last second of it. He fit perfectly in my mouth despite his size and when I swallowed around him he exploded in my mouth. I swallowed every drop, loving that I did that—I made this sexy alpha fall apart with my mouth.

I helped him ride out his orgasm and settled my head on his thigh. "I needed that." I sighed in contentment.

His hand went to my head, just settling there. "Wow."

"Agreed." I crawled up the bed to be by his side.

"Does this mean it's my turn?" He kissed the tip of my nose. "I mean it's not fair that I have all the fun."

"I would argue it was me who had all the fun." I nipped at his bottom lip.

"Guess we will just have to see, won't we?" He kissed me, the taste of him still in my mouth. How could something so small be so incredibly sexy?

Our kiss broke and he started to kiss a similar path down my body, his cock already filling, and by the time he got to my belly, I couldn't wait.

"Dylan, please, I need you inside me." I wasn't above begging.

"Do you mean you need to be inside me… inside my mouth?" He licked me from root to tip. "I can arrange that."

"Yes—no—yes—I'm so slick." My ability to form coherent sentences was gone. "Fill me, alpha mine. I need you."

He settled himself between my legs, grabbing a pillow for under my hips; even in our lust fueled state, he paid attention, took care of me. "This is perfect, omega mine. I can kiss you this way."

I nodded, words not something that were going to happen, reaching around him and pulling his head down to mine, kissing him with all the passion, all the love that I felt.

Our kiss broke, allowing him to line himself up with my slick entrance and ease himself inside. Slowly he moved in and out of me, each stroke an unspoken profession of our connection… our love.

"You feel so good inside of me." I reached up and tweaked his nipple. "Like you were made for me."

"Because I am, my love. I am." His motions sped

up, my hips bucking beneath him, my orgasm rushing forward, not waiting for him to so much as touch my aching cock. My cum shot out between us. Dylan started to lose his rhythm, his climax following quickly behind my own, his knot growing inside of me, connecting us in the most beautiful way as he collapsed on top of me.

"It wasn't a fluke." I hugged him to me, only half joking. It had been my biggest, yet unspoken fear.

"Nope." He nibbled on my earlobe, his breath still bated. "But if you want to be sure, we can keep trying."

"It's not like I'm going to say no to that." I kissed the spot where I longed to mark him.

One day I would.

When it was safe.

Please let that day exist, I thought.

Chapter Seventeen

Dylan

After my knot subsided, I directed my mate to the shower and left him alone for a moment. I wanted to be by his side every minute of every day, but Niko was a strong omega who wasn't used to someone caring about him, much less being with him all of the time. I could tell he needed a minute to decompress and process all that had happened in the last twenty-four hours, our time forgetting about the rest of the world now over. Something had changed after we knotted—like reality set back into him.

I wished I could tuck him into my bed and keep him warm and safe while he rested and rejuvenated. He was due for a good, long sleep to recharge from the pressure he'd been under. Unfortunately, we couldn't rest just yet—we'd already taken more time than we should have.

But he needed that too. We both did. If we were going to be prepared for what was coming, it was necessary to calm our wolves and strengthen our human bond. But that time was over. Now we needed to face reality.

While Niko was in the shower, I worked out a plan. Sure, things looked like they were safe, but knowing what my omega had just shared with me, we weren't and wouldn't be safe until Carter was put down.

My wolf was very on board with that one.

I made several calls, beginning with getting my Betas rounded up and bringing the other omegas to my home. Now that I knew what was coming I no longer felt comfortable with them where they were.

The alpha house was large enough to accommodate all of us, and had the added benefit of being more secluded than the omega dorms. We would need to have a long discussion to bring my Betas up to speed on all that I knew, and we would need the omegas here to tell us more about Shadowpine.

My heart wasn't sure if I could take hearing more about what they went through at the hands of the cruel alphas, but I had to know. We would need to know everything we could about Shadowpine in order to take them down.

I warmed up a plate of food for my omega. My wolf

wanted to make sure he was well-fed and satisfied. I filled the plate with leftover steak, cheesy potatoes, and several dinner rolls. It was carb heavy, but it was comfort food, and I doubted my omega had experienced a lot of that in his short life. I even had dessert ready, chocolate cake with thick fudge frosting.

Niko was just coming down the stairs when I set the plates on the table.

"What's this?" he asked.

"You need to eat." He hadn't put on near the amount of weight that I wanted to see. He was more filled out than when he'd arrived, but his ribs stuck out against his skin and his wrists were bony. I could probably wrap my hand around both his wrists at once.

Niko rolled his eyes. "I've been taking care of myself for my entire life. I can decide when I need to eat." He was definitely back to reality and not the break we managed to get for a short time. I hated that, but also it was necessary.

Gods, I loved his sassiness. We'd never had a dull moment and he wouldn't let me get away with any bullshit. "Humor me," I said. "I just want you to be healthy, and it's been a tough day. There's cake." I pushed a small plate with the slice of chocolate cake that had been delivered.

Niko's stomach rumbled. His tongue darted out to lick his top lip.

Victory for the alpha.

"I am hungry," he said and he sat down. He picked up the fork and pierced the cake. He made a show of taking a bite and giving me a "happy now?" look.

I was. Nothing calmed an alpha wolf faster than seeing his omega well cared for and happy. We had a journey to go on to reach the happiness, but for now taking care of Niko's basic needs would be my top priority. Safety, security, and sustenance.

By the time he finished with his meal, my Betas had arrived with the other omegas in tow, including Cujo, who still wouldn't shift. In the coming days I would need to piece out the rest of the story and what Niko knew of the omegas that followed him. Cujo especially was a mystery, given that none of us ever saw his human form.

We all sat down around the large table.

Lewis and Ralf eyed the empty plate with stray cake crumbs and a bit of frosting, the only evidence left of the dessert that my mate had devoured moments ago.

"There's probably more at the pavilion, if you two would like some," I said.

They ducked their heads. "Thanks, alpha."

Soon I hoped they'd come to treat me like any other member of the pack. I didn't lead by intimidation, and I never wanted to instill fear in the wolves that followed me. Time would have to heal the wounds that had been inflicted on these omegas. My pack and I would be there in whatever way we could to help.

"What's this about?" Piers asked. He rubbed a hand over his belly, shifting in his chair as if trying to find a comfortable position.

Niko lifted his chin. "I told Dylan about Shadowpine."

Kenon, the child, buried his head in Seymour's chest, plastering himself against him. A small whimper escaped his lips and Seymour made comforting shushing noises as he rocked.

"Maybe this conversation would be better if—" Darren started.

Seymour shook his head. "Kenon stays with me." His embrace tightened ever so slightly and the child's hands curled into his father's shirt, holding on for dear life.

I nodded. "All right. I trust you all to make those decisions."

Niko took a deep breath, and I put a hand on his

shoulder, offering my strength as he told his story to my Betas. It had been a shock the first time I heard it, and this time was no different. Darren, Hutch, and Vaughn all got to hear the horrific details for the first time. Their eyes widened and fists clenched with each word Niko said. How a wolf, any wolf, could terrorize omegas in such a way was beyond me.

"Piers and Niko were there before any of us," Seymour said. "My parents died in a fire at my old pack, and no one wanted to take my brother and me in, so when Rowe, one of the Shadowpine alphas, offered to take us in and give them money, my pack jumped at the chance."

Vaughn cursed under his breath and pushed away from the table. He stood, his shoulders tense as he worked to keep his anger under control.

"We weren't allowed to interact a lot. But we did see each other outside. Eventually we began to pass notes, leave messages for each other in the kitchen and laundry areas. When Niko had the plan to escape, we all followed," Seymour said. "Not my brother. He's… he's gone."

No one asked for clarification on that. We all knew what it meant and my wolf cried out at his loss.

"And then we found you," Niko finished, taking the eyes off of Seymour. Niko was a leader, even if he didn't fully see it or want it.

Darren hissed in a breath and swiped at his eyes. Hutch pushed himself to his feet, the wolf inside nearly bursting out. He and Vaughn struggled to maintain composure. Each looked as if they would burst into their fur at any moment to hunt down Shadowpine on their own.

"Sit," I commanded them both. I understood the reaction, but we needed to keep a clear head to gather the information we needed.

Their wolves calmed at the command of their alpha.

Hutch let out a long breath as he finally sat. Sweat beaded on his forehead. "Sorry, alpha," he said. His wolf was still close to the surface, pushing to break free.

"Don't apologize," I said. "It's a natural response. My own was quite similar."

We all had figured it was something along those lines, but hearing it out loud was a shock, to say the least. Knowing the sweet omegas before us had been beaten, brutalized, kept in cages, and treated as slaves was enough to shake even the toughest among us. I planned to make all of Shadowpine pay dearly for the way they treated these omegas. When I was done with them, they'd wish they'd never been born.

"We are going to do everything that we can to keep

you all safe and to take care of Shadowpine once and for all," I vowed, looking at each of them as I spoke. It wasn't just me protecting my omega, we would be protecting all of them.

"How?" Piers asked. "They have so much power and resources. The money the humans pay them… it's a lot. I've seen it. They have to stuff it all in duffel bags to get it from place to place. They have a whole shed at the compound full of it."

I made a note to have each of the omegas give us as much information as possible, including a map of their territory and descriptions of all the alphas. I would need Reeva's advice on how to help them through reliving the trauma. "I don't care what they have," I said. "We're not giving you guys back. You're part of our pack now."

Niko leaned into me. We sat together as one united front. Alpha and omega. It was a small gesture, but large in impact. These omegas followed Niko first, trusted him first, and they may always look to him as their pseudo alpha, but they were Northbay now, and under my protection.

"What do we need to do?" Darren asked.

"The omegas will continue staying in the dorms. They're already settled there, and it's one of the most centrally located buildings. Darren, Hutch, I'll need you to stay there as well." With two Betas there it would be as safe as the pack house. "We'll have extra guards assigned and sentries posted on the border at all times."

I looked at each of the omegas. "We've tried to keep the alphas of the pack away from you until you were more settled, but we'll need them close by for protection." I hated to do this to them, but it was the only way. "I'll command them to give you all as much space as possible. I'm sorry all of you, but shifting and going for a run on your own won't be an option for a while. Not until we know that Shadowpine is gone and it is safe. We don't wish to keep you prisoner—"

"None of us think that," Niko said. He laid a hand on my thigh and squeezed. My wolf howled at the touch and inwardly, I grinned. He was becoming more secure already, showing affection in ways he may have shied away from in the past.

The omegas all nodded in agreement.

"We understand, alpha. Do you think maybe Shadowpine will leave us alone, find other people to occupy their time?" Seymour asked.

"I don't know," I said. "Personally, I would like to have them taken care of in a more permanent way, regardless. Their acts put all shifters at risk, not just wolves. I don't want them torturing other omegas either. Sooner or later they will have to be dealt with."

"You want to kill them?" Piers asked in a hushed tone. The innocence in his eyes was all the more jarring knowing what I knew about him now.

I wanted nothing more to rip them limb from limb, and set them on fire, or perhaps have them drawn and quartered, but I knew that wasn't something these omegas needed to hear and I let his question go unanswered.

"Vaughn, I'll need you to reach out to some of our pack members. Let them know what's going on, and set up a scout schedule."

He nodded. "Yes, alpha."

"Darren, can you take the omegas back to the dorms? You and Hutch can get settled there. Niko will be staying at the alpha house with me."

"Wouldn't it make the most sense to keep them all together?" Hutch said, and I shot him a look.

He bared his neck. "Of course, alpha."

"Tomorrow, first thing, we're going to have to sit down and have some questions answered. We'll need to know everything there is to know about Shadowpine." The fear in the room became palpable. If there were any way around putting them through that I would do it, but there wasn't. This was life or death—theirs.

"Things like who they are, how many live there,

and what they look like. Anything you can tell us will be helpful in tracking them down, or recognizing them if they appear here. I know it will be hard to dredge that all up, but it will be necessary. We can have Ilyssa or Reeva sit down and talk with you all if that would be more comfortable." They had both built a bond with the omegas over their time here and it wouldn't make it better, but maybe it might help.

Seymour, Piers, Lewis, and Ralf all nodded at me. They still looked to Niko for confirmation. They likely always would.

"If there's anything you all need," I said, looking at each of the omegas individually, including Cujo in wolf form. "Do not hesitate to let us know. You are Northbay now." I would need to make it official, but at the end of the day they were mine to protect, ceremony or no.

Seymour held Kenon, who'd fallen asleep during the conversation. Lewis and Ralf held hands and leaned against each other. Piers sniffled. The air around them was heavy with fatigue and worry, but there was hope present as well. In time it would grow to overshadow the fear.

They all stood and followed Darren and Hutch out the door. Piers hugged his brother before he left, whispering something into his ear.

Once they were out of the room, I let out a long

breath and pulled Niko into my arms. The tension in his thin frame melted away in my embrace.

“I should be with them,” he said.

“Do you want to go with them right now? I won’t keep you from them if that is where you want to be.”

Stay, my wolf disagreed.

“Soon,” he said. “I’ll visit them for a while, but first I just want to be here with you. I'm tired. We've been running for so long that it seems weird to rely on anyone else. I'm not used to it.”

I tucked a finger under his chin, and lifted his gaze to mine. I kissed his lips. “Let me take care of you, omega. We're here for you now. You aren't alone. You all have us now.”

He smiled at me, and it was as if a ray of sunshine lit up the room. “Thank you, alpha mine.”

Chapter Eighteen

Niko

Not being with my brother turned out to be far more difficult than I imagined. I wanted to be with him—to protect him. But also, I understood why Dylan wanted me here with him. His home was his personal territory and his wolf wanted me there. The pack house back at Shadowpine was where evil happened, and this pack house was a far cry from that.

The first night, I almost left to be back with my brother and the other omegas. I felt completely safe and cocooned in my new home with Dylan. It wasn't that. It was a sense of guilt for leaving them. They'd been my responsibility for so long and I felt as if I was failing them by not being with them.

My wolf wouldn't let me leave the pack house though, taking my skin from me and curling up on the bed with my mate. He'd been right. Of course he had.

The next day I sat down with them all at the omega dorms and we discussed my conflicted feelings. I don't know what I was expecting, but it wasn't Piers telling me how my becoming the Alpha Omega gave them hope that all would work out or Seymour telling me I made his son's future possible or the twins hugging me tightly and making me promise to accept Dylan's love and to know that I was worthy.

Even Cujo surprised me, by licking my face.

They were happy for me and wanted me to have the life being offered me. And that made things easier. Sure, I still missed my brother like crazy, but it no longer came with a shroud of guilt.

It helped when Dylan gave us all what he called cell phones and showed me that I could call or send messages to them. Why I would ever need to use the device when I could just walk over to the dorms was beyond me, but I appreciated the gesture.

"What has you so deep in thought, mate?" Dylan set a mug of coffee in front of me. Gods, I loved it when he called me that. He must too. It was rare when he called me Niko and when he did it was often Niko, omega mine, not plain Niko.

"The whole Alpha Omega thing," I admitted. "Like I understand it's a thing, but also—it's never really been one where I've lived." My home pack—our Alpha Omega was gone long before my memories started. I never heard the story of why, but looking back there was a reason it wasn't offered. And in Shadowpine? The notion that an omega had any slight bit of power was almost laughable. Omegas were property. Full. Stop.

"What if… your pack deserves someone who understands the role." And wasn't being hunted by a sadist. Because there was that, too. But that I couldn't change. My ability to fill the shoes given to me? That I could work on.

"There's no right way to be the Alpha Omega." He sat beside me, placing his hand on my own. "My parents weren't the best pair to be in this house. They weren't harmful, but also—"

"But your grandparents." I had not a stitch of doubt Gramps was a kick ass Alpha if there ever was one.

"That's my point, sort of…" he leaned his head on my shoulder.

"That makes no sense." I wanted it to. I wanted all of this to make sense.

"You will be amazing." It still didn't make sense, but the sincerity in his words told me he believed it… believed in me.

"I'm headstrong." Understatement of the year and my wolf—even more so than myself.

"I know." He chuckled as if it were something good

and slightly amusing and not a pain in the butt.

"And I can be sassy."

"I love that side of you. It means you feel safe and comfortable." I wasn't sure that was true.

My rebellious side had historically been a way of keeping my brother safe, sure. Piss off the alpha and he forgets about the others kind of thing. But since I was here—maybe Dylan was right. Maybe now that I no longer needed it to protect, maybe now it was coming out in the fun way.

Gods, could I over think things anymore?

"I don't know what to do." Or even what I was expected to do.

"That's simple—you already do it." His arm came around behind me, gently easing him even closer to him. "It's natural for you. Look how you pulled the omegas together against all odds, brought them here, and the entire time kept them feeling like things were going to work out even when skies were the darkest. That was what they needed and you instinctively knew that."

"It's what had to happen," I countered. "Anyone would have done it."

"Ahh, but that's what you don't see—others wouldn't have, not from lack of desire but because they wouldn't even begin to see what was needed.

Trust me, omega mine. The Northbay pack is honored to have you. I am honored to have you by my side. You make me a better alpha."

"You were the alpha who took us in when so many would've either turned us away or contacted our owners. You don't give yourself enough credit."

The toaster dinged. "I'll get that. No one wants cold toast." I hopped up and over to the toaster, glad for the break in heavy conversation. "Cinnamon raisin toast is the best."

We'd already eaten breakfast, but when Reeva dropped off a loaf of homemade raisin bread, it instantly became snack time.

Someone knocked at the door and my stomach dropped. I was looking forward to the day when that would no longer happen. I didn't want to be hesitant and scared when pack members stopped by. "I'll see who it is." Dylan went off to answer it as I slathered our toast with butter.

"Is that for me?" Gramps stood in the doorway. "If my nose is worth anything, that's Reeva's bread."

"It is and yes, this one's for you." I walked around with two plates, handing one to him and one to my mate. "And this is for you." I went back to make more, because as much as I'd like to say I'd sacrifice my toast for company, that wasn't the case. It smelled too good.

"Will anyone want more?" I asked as I stepped lively over to the toaster to refill it.

They both were too busy inhaling their toast to answer and I took that as a *please fill the toaster.*

"So what brings you here, grandfather?" Dylan spoke, his mouth full. "Need something done at your place?"

"Hardly. Your mate is downright handy." He winked at me. "You should probably keep him."

"Huh." Dylan smooshed his face to one side. "I probably should, I suppose."

I stuck my tongue out at both of them.

"Speaking of your mate, I came to borrow yours," Gramps said. "I'll bring him back tonight."

"I'll walk you guys back. I need to check in with Darren anyway." Dylan popped the last bit of his toast in my mouth.

"Or maybe *he* has plans for the day." The toaster popped and I went to buttering my toast as Gramps chuckled. "Maybe I will eat this all." I wasn't opposed to the idea.

"Niko, would you like to come over for a bit? I have a project I could use some help on." Gramps contained his laughter. "And if you want to eat it all, that is fine. An old man like me doesn't need the simple pleasures in life."

I rolled my eyes and held out a buttered piece to him. "This is because I made it for you, not because your performance was fabulous. If anything, I'd say it was a three out of ten."

I handed Dylan a piece as well and took a huge bite of mine.

"It wasn't your best, Grandfather," Dylan agreed with me.

"You taking his side?" Gramps teased.

"He's better looking." Dylan gave it right back. "And besides—he's the keeper of the toast."

"I am the keeper of the toast." I took another bite, loving the melty buttery goodness paired with the cinnamon. "And Gramps, I'd love to come help you with your project."

"Why does he get to call you Gramps?" Dylan attempted to side eye his grandfather, instead accomplishing nothing other than making a silly face.

"Because he's better looking… and the keeper of the toast."

"And here I was thinking that I had big shoes to fill by becoming the Alpha Omega and really I should've been worried about my task as keeper of the toast." I grabbed the butter off the counter and put it back in the fridge.

"It is an important job." Gramps rubbed his chin.

"In all seriousness, is now a good time?"

"It is perfect." Dylan hugged his grandfather. I loved seeing this side of him… the silly, playful, grandson and mate side where for a sliver of time he wasn't Alpha capital A. He was just Dylan.

And there was no just to it. Dylan was far more than enough.

True to his word, Dylan walked us to his grandfather's place.

"He's protective," I said as soon as the door clicked shut.

"I was the same with my Earl. It is the way of things." Gramps shrugged. "Ready to get to work?"

"Sure. What are we doing?" I'd never thought to ask. It didn't really matter. I loved helping him around the place.

"Follow me." He took me upstairs, where he pulled the latch on the ceiling to bring down the attic stairs. I'd been in the place so many times and never once had I noticed it before. "We need to get some things from here."

The rickety stairs led to a surprisingly finished attic filled with boxes and furniture.

"Your brother is getting rounder with each day," he noted. "He's going to be needing some things."

"I was going to ask Reeva about how they handle that in the pack." In the pack I grew up in they sort of passed things from one person to the next. In Shadowpine—I didn't even want to go there.

"Reeva will help him get connected with diapers and such, but that wasn't what I was thinking about." He moved a few boxes and then dragged out a cradle from behind the pile.

"My Earl made this. I used it with my son and he used it with his boys… I want your brother to use it for his child."

I blinked away the tears at such complete acceptance of not only me, but those I brought with me. "It's beautiful."

"It needs work and that's what I need you for today, but it is gorgeous." He blew away some of the dust. "Every plane was meticulously made by hand and with so much love. And don't think I am passing you by." My eyes must've gone wide because he quickly added on, "I mean for your babes… I'm not skipping you over. Dylan's brother is a master woodworker and he will want to be the one to make it for you."

Gramps stepped over. "Why are you green?"

"I… I… I might not be able to carry young," I confessed, my stomach about to revolt. It was one thing for Dylan to be okay with it. But for a grandfather to see his legacy slip away... that was altogether a different story.

"Then he'll probably make you a porch swing or an end table or something." It was as if he hadn't even heard what I said. "You are family and valued not because of what you can give us, but by what you have already given my grandson—his fated mate," he explained. "Now help me get this downstairs. It needs a good old fashioned scrubbing and possibly to be refinished, and knowing Dylan he'll be back here in an hour missing you something fierce."

He wasn't wrong. Dylan showed up shortly after we had it scrubbed down and ready to refinish. He helped us as Gramps regaled us with stories about the crib from its start as a fallen log Earl thought was too good to waste to Dylan's father spitting up all over it the very first time he was laid in it. We laughed, groaned, and worked together in the way I always dreamed a pack should.

Only this wasn't a dream.

This was a pack.

My pack.

And these—these people were my family.

Maybe I was dreaming after all.

Chapter Nineteen

Dylan

My mate and I were minding our own damn business, relaxing on the couch, when the door was pushed open. I had been showing Niko how to navigate the movie streaming app, so he could enjoy some entertainment, but so far he was mostly confused why anyone bothered to film things that weren't real.

"Why don't they just tell the stories out loud?" he asked.

"Well, this way people can enjoy them in their own homes."

"What's the message? Are there morals to these stories, lessons that the young humans can learn?"

I stared at the TV screen where two dudes with wild hair were depicted, one pulling his hair, the other pulling his ears. "No, not always. Sometimes it's just funny." Sometimes they were just dumb.

"I don't get it," Niko said.

"That's okay, you don't have to."

Perhaps the human experience of cinematic enjoyment would be a lesson for another day.

The door creaked open and I immediately bolted to my feet, halfway shifting to my wolf form, a growl erupting from my lips. Niko was right at my side. He was never one to sit back and hide when a fight was taking place. He was ready for a fight as well.

Thankfully, the scent of my brother and his mate reached my nose before I could pounce.

Ozzy walked into the living room, his daughter Zoey in his arms. "What's up, brother? Is this how you greet all your guests?"

I relaxed immediately, my claws retracting and canines returning to my regular human teeth so I could smile at my niece without scaring her. Niko looked between me and Ozzy.

I put my arm around his shoulders. "Mate. This is my brother, Ozzy."

Ozzy's eyebrows rose. "You found your mate?" His voice softened and went all high pitched and squealy. He closed the space between himself and Niko and put his arms around Niko, embracing him in a hug.

Niko just stood there, looking at me wide-eyed. He

patted Ozzy's back awkwardly while Ozzy rocked him back and forth. Zoey seemed uninterested. Her eyes were on me, her favorite uncle.

I shrugged. I was just as surprised as Niko was, since Ozzy wasn't usually the touchy feely type.

Ozzy stepped back and wiped his eyes. "Sorry, I get emotional when I'm pregnant."

"Pregnant?" I said. I'd thought the two of them would wait a little longer before having a second pup, though I was happy to be an uncle again. I doted on my niece.

I took Zoey from his arms and made funny faces at her. "Since when is your daddy pregnant?" Zoey giggled and squirmed. She reached for my cheeks and slapped them playfully with her little hands.

"It happened a few weeks ago," he said. "Kade and I were—"

"Lalalalala. I don't need details," I said. "I just meant, how far along are you?"

Ozzy rolled his eyes. "It's early yet. We've barely told the pack."

"Congratulations, brother." I gave Ozzy an awkward side-hug, now that he'd let my mate go.

"Thanks."

He looked at Niko and then back at me. "So are you

gonna fill me in on the story here or…"

"I'm Niko." Niko held out his hand and Ozzy shook it. "Me and some of my friends are soon to be pack members." I hated the soon to be part. They were in every way that counted. A ceremony didn't make them any more so, it just had them scented like us.

Me and my friends are soon to be pack members. That was about as tame as he could possibly put it. I would need to fill in Ozzy and Kade, and then have Kade fill in Byrom. It wasn't necessarily any of their business, but I also didn't need rumors flying about why we were picking a fight with the Shadowpine pack. When push came to shove, I knew I had Byrom and Greycoast's trust and they would have our backs. In return, I could at least tell them the whole story.

It also made them safer to know just in case their territory got breached.

"Ozzy, am I carrying this thing in or what do you want me to do with it?" Kade, Ozzy's mate, called from somewhere outside.

"Oh yeah! I came with gifts," Ozzy beamed.

We went outside to find Kade standing on the porch with three massive shelves.

"What in the world am I supposed to do with those?" I said. "My office has plenty of shelves. I can't fit anymore."

"They're not for you, they're for Reeva. They mentioned needing to reorganize their medications and I thought this would be perfect. This setup worked well for our healer, so I put together an extra set."

"So why are they here at my house?" I asked.

"Reeva doesn't have room yet, and your house is huge and empty so you can store them until Reeva is ready. Geesh, do I have to explain everything." He kinda did.

I rolled my eyes. If it was up to me the house wouldn't be empty for long. "All right, let's bring them in."

I handed my niece to Niko. He had a panicked look before he took the child in his arms. She looked up at him with her sweet blue eyes sparkling. She would have him wrapped around her paw in no time. Niko would love her, I'd seen how he was with Kenon. He had a gift with children.

I helped Kade maneuver all three bookshelves into the house. We stored them in one of the empty bedrooms.

"Are you guys going to stay for a visit?" I asked when we returned to the living room. "I'd really like if you could get to know Niko a little better." Niko was on the floor with Zoey, while Ozzy sat on the couch.

"Of course," Kade said. "We had no idea you were

even mated."

I chuckled. "It's recent." Hell, it had only been a few days. "A lot has happened and I haven't had a chance to call."

"Oh! Can we stay for dinner? I've been craving Sarah's meatloaf for ages now. Kade's recipe just isn't the same."

"I try," Kade whined.

I gave him a playful shove. "You not taking good care of my brother, Kade? Remember what I said would happen if I found out you weren't taking good care of him." I winked at my mate, to make sure he knew we were playing.

He grinned back at me. Zoey had crawled into his lap. She tugged at the strings to his hoodie. The contentedness and ease at which he fit into my family made my heart squeeze. These were the moments I'd wanted forever and now I had them.

I picked up the phone, about to order some food from the pavilion, when the door burst open again.

"Alpha!" Ilyssa came running into the house. I didn't like the fear that I heard in her voice and saw in her eyes.

"What is it?" I asked.

"We have visitors on the south end of the territory, right along the main road. They're driving a truck."

"How many?" I asked.

"Just one. Dark black hair, blue eyes. Scary."

Niko sucked in a breath. "That's Carter."

My wolf howled, ready for a fight, ready to take down the alpha that had tortured my mate.

"Ozzy, go with Niko to the Omega dorms. Niko, let Darren know why you're there and send Vaughn to the front gate with me."

He nodded and they both scrambled to their feet. Zoey reached for her daddy and Ozzy took her back into his arms. Niko kissed my cheek before ushering Ozzy out the door.

"Something I should know about?" Kade asked once they were out of earshot.

"I can fill you in later. We don't like this Carter guy."

He nodded. "Got it."

Being a Beta of his own pack, Kade knew how to follow an Alpha's lead. He flanked my side along with Vaughn and Hutch. We opted to take our ATVs to the entrance off the main road rather than meet as wolves. If Carter was arriving in a truck, he wasn't here to attack. If humans passed by a group of men standing around in the nude, it'd draw suspicion.

When we reached the main gate, the man I now knew was Carter leaned against a slick black truck. His arms were folded over his chest, covered by a leather jacket. He wore a dark pair of jeans. The tip of his left ear was missing, like the wolf Leah had seen on the night of the full moon. So it had been him trespassing on my pack lands.

"Alpha," he said and bared his neck ever so slightly. It was enough for me to notice, and acknowledge, but not enough that I felt it was legitimate.

"You're not welcome here," I said.

He chuckled. "Do you even know why I'm here?"

"I can venture a guess." I wasn't about to give away what I knew about him or his intentions toward my omega, but I would be clear about my intentions toward him. He wasn't welcome, and he needed to know that. It took everything I had not to tear him apart, given what I knew about what he'd done to my mate. But attacking first, without provocation wouldn't go over well.

Carter leaned slightly toward me and sniffed. His nostrils flared and recognition registered in his eyes.

"Is that the way it's going to be?" He stood straight, his shoulders tensed as if he was prepared to launch at me. I remained where I was. "You don't know who you're messing with." He cracked his knuckles.

I smirked. "You don't scare me," I said.

"That omega, and those that follow him, will only bring you trouble, like they have for me. Let me take them off your hands." He spoke so nonchalantly, as if he was talking about a pet cat and not real people.

"If they're so much trouble you won't mind if they stay here with me," I said. "They are Northbay now. And we take care of our own."

"I'm a reasonable man. I can negotiate. Give me the older brother. You can keep the pregnant omega. He isn't likely to bear an alpha son and he's too weak for my purposes anyway." Carter stood at his full height now, his chin tipped up in an attempt to tower over me.

I wasn't intimidated. I shook my head. "Never going to happen. You can't have either of them." He hadn't mentioned Seymour or the others; perhaps he didn't know that they'd all stuck together. Given that he had no concept of loyalty, that didn't surprise me.

He smiled, his eyes turning dark. "Fine. Give me the pregnant one, if you're so fond of the older one. Surely you don't want another mouth to feed around here. You all look like you're practically wasting away and starving. You live so… primitively."

We were no such thing and he knew it. My wolf growled; our patience with this game was wearing thin. The fastest way to piss off an alpha was to belittle his pack.

Behind me, Vaughn and Hutch squared their feet.

"Leave now," I said, my voice rising. "You are not welcome here. You will not be getting either of the omegas. You're lucky we don't tear you apart right now after what you did to them." My wolf wanted me to do just that.

"The other alphas in Shadowpine won't be pleased to hear this," he said. "There will be trouble."

"If they cared, they'd be here now to help gather the brothers. But they aren't. I'm guessing you're here on your own and the others in Shadowpine don't care about getting them back." It was just a guess, but I hit my mark.

Carter's eyes flicked away from me and he flinched ever so slightly. He was here without back up. The rest of Shadowpine had given up on the omegas; likely they had found new ones to torture, but Carter wanted Niko and Piers and he wasn't ready to let them go.

"Leave," I said again.

"This isn't over," he threatened as he slunk away into his truck and left.

"Care to fill me in?" Kade asked once we no longer saw the truck's taillights.

I did as best as I could and explained about Shadowpine, and what they did to the omegas that were now in my care. I only gave as much information as Kade needed to know. I didn't wish to recount the entire story any more than I had to.

"Whoof." Kade let out a long breath. "I'll talk with Byrom. He'll offer any assistance you need. How are they all? Physically and mentally?"

I nodded. "We would appreciate that. They're recovering well. Still a bit wary of us, but coming along nicely. It'll take time."

"Thank goodness Niko and his omegas came here when they did, and had an alpha like you to watch out for them." Kade patted me on the shoulder. "And you found your mate too. Seems like fate had your back."

"Something like that," I said. "Kinda like how me sending my brother to Greycoast was like fate for you."

"Exactly. Let's go back. I heard there's meatloaf and my omega is going to want to know everything."

We piled back on the ATVs and took off toward the houses. This wasn't over yet, but it would be soon. The next time I saw Carter, he wasn't going to walk away alive. I just hoped to gods that letting him walk away this time hadn't been a deadly mistake, but having his entire pack coming to look for him wasn't a risk I was willing to make until we were ready… whatever that looked like.

Chapter Twenty

Niko

By Dylan's description of all that had transpired, it was definitely Carter that came to visit. He wasn't one to do his own dirty work and I had a dozen scenarios running through my brain while he was gone. I wanted to go and sniff it out to know for sure, but Dylan was having no part of me going anywhere near there and the other alphas all agreed. Heck, even the omegas agreed. No one wanted me there and I got it. Carter was after my brother and me.

And in a sick way, that filled me with some relief. Maybe they didn't know Cujo, the twins, Seymour, and Kenon were all with us. They knew some, but maybe… just maybe some of them were completely safe from the hunt. And make no mistake about it. It was a hunt. Had it been anything else, they'd have already been here guns blazing, because unlike a true wolf, these bastards used human weapons.

They thought it made them powerful.

All it did was show how weak and cowardly they were.

It had been a week and not a word. Some of the guys thought that was a good sign. I knew better. It meant they were planning and organizing. Had they rushed in we'd have stood a much better chance of no one in our pack being hurt. An organized and weaponized Shadowpine pack—I quivered at the thought of it.

Dylan seemed to believe that Carter was operating on his own, that the rest of Shadowpine had forgotten us. I hoped that was true.

"I'm just going to see Reeva," I told Darren. If Dylan wasn't by my side, one of his Betas was. And I wasn't even close to exaggerating. If I so much as stepped out onto the porch, I had a shadow. We all did.

"Cool. I haven't seen Reeva in a week." He acted like I'd just told him we were going to see Santa and not like I told him he was going to have to accompany my butt to the healer's.

We didn't chat along the way. We never did when out in the open like this. And that wasn't a Darren thing. That was a "just the way it was thing." Their wolves were always on high alert making sure I was safe—that all the omegas were safe.

I hated that this was their lives because of me. So many times I wished that I had killed Carter on our way out. Gods knew I had dreamt about killing him so many times.

But what would that have done? If he was dead, Rowe would come looking. If I managed to get both of them, Edgar would have come, and the list went on and on unless I had decimated the entire pack. That was a mission I couldn't come close to accomplishing.

Not that I thought I'd be any match for Edgar. He was the worst of what Shadowpine had to offer. Cujo had been his, and none of us knew what had transpired between the two.

"Should've asked if you were feeling okay." Darren let out a long breath as we reached the steps, an audible sigh of relief. "I mean, you are going to Reeva's." He pinched the bridge of his nose.

"Don't worry about it. You had—you had a job to do and it didn't include small talk."

"Are you okay?" he asked.

"I'm here to help mount and possibly stock some of the shelves for Reeva. Ozzy brought them over from Greycoast and they've been just sitting there. Piers saw them at his visit." Darren relaxed slightly.

"I'm glad." He scratched his forehead. "Need help?"

"Probably. I didn't actually get a good look at them, even though I was there when Ozzy and Kade brought them. I was preoccupied with Zoey, but Piers said they were and I quote, *fancy,* so they could be small and ornate or huge with multiple levels. You never know with him."

Reeva opened the door and welcomed us, and we were greeted by the scent of something baking.

"Came to the right place." Darren rubbed his belly.

"The cookies are for helpers," Reeva said with a smile. "Little Red Hen style." They wore a pair of overalls, with their hair pulled back and tucked under a bandana.

"Good thing I came to help," I said. "I'm pretty sure Kenon sent me his strength to help." I flexed my muscles the way he did when he was showing he was strong. "He may need me to bring him home some cookies."

"Kenon already has a plate set aside. He is a gift this pack has yet to truly realize." Reeva walked into the next room, not clarifying whatever they meant by that.

I looked to Darren, who just shrugged. He was probably used to Reeva's manner of being overly blunt but also cryptic.

"Let's go take care of these shelves and Darren,

thanks for… I don't know… treating us like we belong, I guess." For whatever reason I was feeling a bit more emotional than normal. I had a feeling it was more to do with finally belonging than anything else, but part of me wondered if it could be something more—something I was scared to even consider for fear of being wrong.

We followed Reeva, who had already moved everything away from the far wall. "This is where I think they belong."

"Think?" I would put them up and down ten times if they asked. They'd saved my brother and my niece or nephew. I owed them so much. But it was probably best not to make too many holes in the wall.

"It makes sense to be over there." Reeva pointed to the wall now piled high with boxes. "But I think it belongs here." They rubbed their chin. "So here it is."

"And where are they?" Darren asked.

"Oh right, come this way." We followed them out into the adjoining room. This wasn't just a couple of little shelves for knick-knacks or jars. Nope. Ozzy had built the most stunning shelves that would pretty much cover the entire wall. It was going to be gorgeous. Absolutely gorgeous.

And a lot more work than I had thought, which was

good. I needed to keep busy. "Ozzy has so much talent." I ran my fingers down the curve of the trim.

"He has many," Darren spoke fondly. "Looks like we best make a start."

We spent the next two hours measuring, bracing, and hanging the shelves. The three of us worked in tandem. It was nice. Like being pack made us equal even if I wasn't *officially* pack just yet. It was something I'd never experienced before coming here and was something I was excited Piers's young would have.

"Do you want help putting things back on the shelf or have we earned our cookies?" Darren asked as he emptied the dust pan, marking the end of our final step in shelf mounting.

"As much as I would love help stocking, you two wouldn't know where things went and it is easiest if I do it myself." They waved us over. "Now let's get you some cookies and tea."

They didn't have to ask us twice.

Reeva had to have gotten up at three am to make all the cookies set before us. There were sugar cookies, oatmeal cookies, and my favorite, chocolate chip. We stood at the counter and ate and ate, all pretense of manners out the window. We worked hard and cookies. 'Nuff said.

"Can you help me for a second, Niko?" Reeva set

two mugs of tea down. "I need something from the other room."

"I can—" Reeva shut Darren down with a glance. What was I missing?

As we stepped out of the room, I discovered what we were missing quickly enough—and it wasn't a tea cup.

"I hope you're drinking milk and eating enough protein." Reeva started to rummage around in a box they had packed up.

"I don't really like milk that much." It wasn't a part of my regular diet, but I wasn't opposed to it. "But I eat well—better than I ever had before." And not out of lack of desire. We just were fed scraps. Done.

"The milk isn't for you." They pulled out a vial. "This will do." They handed it to me. "Three drops in your milk each morning and it should keep your tummy better throughout the day."

"My tummy is fine." I went to hand it back.

"But it won't be for long." Reeva rolled their eyes. "Babies tend to mess with them and this will help."

The milk isn't for you.

"You think I'm pregnant?" I gasped, finally connecting the dots.

"You are pregnant. Did you not know?" They

looked at me bewildered.

"Babies—they—I'm not pregnant." I mean, I thought maybe, but I pushed it so far down, extinguishing the spark of hope. I couldn't handle the disappointment. It would be one thing too many.

"You are. I feel them." Reeva pushed my hand closed around the vial. "You are having a baby."

"I am having a baby!" I said a bit too loudly, and from the cough in the next room, Darren had heard. "Are you sure?"

"It's kind of my job." They rolled their eyes. "Drink your milk. Use this. And don't skimp on the protein."

"I'm having a baby," I whispered. I put a hand over my flat stomach. Inside a tiny pup grew. One that was both Dylan and I.

"Yes, now go drink your tea. I added extra ginger to it. You'll thank me after eating all those cookies. Prop yourself up on extra pillows at night if the reflux gets too bad, okay? We'll set you up with some regular appointments starting next week."

I went back to the kitchen and drank my tea slowly, trying to digest all Reeva had said. Darren just stared at me as if he were unsure what to say or do. Which was fair enough since I was unsure what to say or do.

I was pregnant, the most amazing news ever. But also—Carter was after me. The timing was—

Babe. My wolf finally caught up to what was going on. Took him long enough.

Mate. Babe. Mate.

Yes, we did need to tell Dylan soon.

"Darren, do you know when Dylan is going to be done for the day?" Any attempt I had of being chill fell on its face, my voice almost squeaking by the end of the sentence.

"I don't, but he is going to be pleased." Darren snapped his mouth shut.

"I knew you heard." I brought my mug to the sink and directed my attention to Reeva. "Any chance of snagging a few for my brother?" I indicated the cookies.

Reeva chuckled. "See that box." They pointed to one on the far side of the counter. "Those are the cookies for the omega dorms. Kenon's are shaped like animals in a special dish—it will be clear."

"You're the best." I went for the box. "Thanks for everything."

"Says the man who helped mount my shelves."

We said our goodbyes and Darren immediately reached for the box.

"I got it." I might be an omega, but I was strong enough to carry cookies.

"But the…"

"I'm pregnant, not sick, and besides, if I need protecting you need to be able to shift without worrying about cookies." That had him reluctantly agreeing.

We walked mostly in silence, but as we rounded the corner to the omega house he said, "I can't lie to Dylan."

"I would never ask you to, and it's not like he would ask you how the day went and you'd have to blurt out *your omega's pregnant*." For some reason that amused me.

"I know, but I'm new and I don't want to mess up," he confessed.

"You won't, and even if you did, Dylan sees you as the wolf he needs by his side." I caught a glimpse of Seymour glancing out the window. "And besides—I'll be the one blurting it out. Let's get inside, they're probably waiting."

And sure enough everyone was in the common area pretending they hadn't been watching the door.

"Reeva sent cookies." I set the box on the coffee table. "Sorry it took so long."

"We just…" Piers stopped mid-sentence.

"The shelves weren't tiny," I explained. I could see why they'd been worried. Every one of us had been on alert since the run-in with Shadowpine. "I did get some good news."

Part of me said I should wait for Dylan, but a bigger part of me wanted help telling Dylan. This news was big, and even if the timing was less than ideal, I wanted to celebrate it. It had to be spectacular.

"And I need your help telling Dylan." I settled my hands on my belly and watched as Piers pieced it together.

Lewis jumped up and nearly tackle-hugged me. Seymour gasped, bringing his hands to his mouth, his eyes filled with so much joy. Ralf was mumbling something about knowing it already. And Piers? He just sat there with the largest smile I'd ever seen on him in all our years. Larger than even when things weren't that bad. Because until recently, they were never good.

"Why do you need help?" Darren asked when the commotion ended. "Are you… is there…"

I nipped whatever negative worry he had in the bud. "Because, my friend, it's fun. You wouldn't know this but I… I never thought I could carry his young and this is a huge deal. I want to celebrate it as such."

His mouth formed an O.

"This will be fun." Seymour got up off the couch, Kenon still sitting there half asleep. "I never—we never got to celebrate our babies… this will be fabulous."

I desperately hoped that each of them found their alpha some day, like how I had found mine. There were lots of alphas in Northbay; it was likely their mates were out there.

"Does that mean you have an idea?" Because aside from blurting out I was pregnant, I sure didn't.

Cujo jumped on the couch and sat next to Kenon, who snuggled into him like he was a pillow.

"I might." Darren's lip curled into a smile. "We'll have to call Ozzy."

Chapter Twenty-One

Dylan

Coming home from a long day of work, knowing that my omega was at my house, waiting for me, was a dream come true. I hadn't realized just how much I was missing from my life until Niko was there to fill the void. He was there when I needed to talk, to bounce things off him for the pack. He was filled with the best ideas for pack activities, and we were beyond excited to share them with the pack.

Most days Niko was out and about amongst the pack with me. Now that he felt more comfortable among us and some trust had been built, he met each and every pack member. Many times he would sit with them for hours to hear their stories. He knew more about pack history now than I did. When he did stay home, his omegas visited him. I had even arrived home once to find some of the other younger omegas talking with him and seeking his guidance.

Niko was fulfilling the role of Alpha Omega for the pack without even realizing it. I loved that, loved him.

I came home from the last roofing job we had. We'd spent the last several hours hanging gutters on the side of my grandfather's house. My arms were aching, and my body hurt in ways I didn't know that it could, but the job was done and I was happy to not have to worry about roofing for at least another decade.

It was another way that I provided for my pack and improved their lives. We took care of all our pack members, especially our elderly. I couldn't wait to tell my omega that we were finally finished with the huge undertaking.

I knew my grandfather had been complaining to Niko that the roofing crew was making too much noise. I half suspected it was just an excuse to come visit him. My grandfather cherished my omega and not just because he was my mate. They had a beautiful bond that brought light into the life of the lonely old man.

When I walked inside, there was music playing from somewhere in the house, but I couldn't quite pinpoint it. Since my omega had gotten his own cell phone, he had turned to liking several things about it, including having music playing at all times. At first he thought it silly and a waste, but now? Now he was loving it. I was happy that he had found something that he enjoyed, something that was just his. He never had understood the purpose of movies enough to enjoy them. I could sort of see his point.

I went to the steps and followed the noise to one of these spare bedrooms. It was one of the smaller ones that had an adjoining door to the master bedroom, where the Alpha Omega and I stayed. Niko was on the floor, a box of old toys in front of him and an old rocking chair sitting in the corner. This morning when I had left, this room had been empty.

I'd thought about turning it into a reading nook or possibly a private sitting area but it never felt right. Like the room had a purpose and I just needed to be patient to discover what that purpose was.

"What's going on?" I said.

Niko looked up. He held a toy duck in his hands that had been hand carved by my grandfather. The yellow paint was chipped and there were a few dings on the toy, but I had no doubt that it could be refinished and like new again. I didn't have the woodworking skills that Ozzy had, but I could fix things.

Niko grinned up at me. "How was your day?" he asked, avoiding my question.

"Great. You seem very happy."

He sat cross-legged on the floor, his knees bouncing as if he couldn't contain his excitement or perhaps had too many cups of coffee. Once I introduced him to flavored creamer, he'd been drinking coffee like it was his job. Yet another luxury that he relished in, that I had taken for granted my whole life. "I am," he beamed up at me.

Nothing made my wolf happier. "Were you able to help Reeva get the shelves set up?"

Niko nodded. "Yep, Darren did all the heavy lifting for us."

I snorted. "Yeah, he got out of all the hard work of hanging the gutters on that old house of my grand-father's. Lucky wolf." He'd have done the roofing in a heartbeat, but there was a reason I wanted him with the omegas. He understood being new and also understood how bad things could get. He'd seen evil first hand. My wolf trusted him completely to keep them safe.

"The shelves are stunning." He kept his eyes on the duck. "Your brother is beyond gifted. Reeva sent cookies."

"The kind with the pecans?" They were my favorite.

"Reeva sent so many kinds I don't even know." Niko bit his lip and looked up at me through low-ered lashes. "I started to feel a little off while I was at Reeva's."

"Oh really?" I tipped my head to the side. "What happened? Did you drink too much coffee after I left? It can make you really jittery, like you're going to bounce out of your skin." If he wasn't bouncing with happiness I'd have worried he might be coming down with something.

Maybe he was bouncing with coffee.

"No, coffee wouldn't betray me like that," he sassed. "I got a bit emotional is all and I thought it was odd." Nothing odd about being emotional given all they had gone through. "And tiredness, a little lightheaded feeling… hunger."

My brow furrowed and my wolf perked. He didn't like the sound of our omega not feeling well. But also, Niko wasn't sounding like there was anything to worry about… like maybe it was good?

"Did you eat enough?" Thinking back, he didn't eat all of his bacon in the morning, which… bacon. "Drink enough water and not just coffee?" I don't know why I bothered with that question. Of course he didn't. All the coffee all the time.

He looked up at me with a grin.

"Are you alright?" I couldn't figure out if I was supposed to be worried or not and why he was in this room, and I was definitely missing something.

"I'm fine. Reeva explained, so it's fine." He shrugged. "But I had to call your brother."

"My brother? Why? Was there an issue with the shelving?"

Niko's grin widened. "I needed his advice, but not on the shelving. I wasn't sure what supplies we all had, for…" He trailed off and made a sweeping gesture around the room.

I stepped into the room, looking carefully at all of the things he must have brought down from the attic. I vaguely remembered seeing these items up there when I'd packed away the last of my parents' things when they moved out. I hoped Niko had not done this all himself and instead had Darren help with the heavy stuff.

There were baby clothes and toys and a rocking chair. If only we had a crib, this could be a full nursery. A nursery. Like for a…

"Are you…?"

Niko stood and grinned at me. "According to Reeva, who I trust very much, we're gonna have a baby." He squealed out the words as the happiness bubbled out of him.

I wrapped my arms around him and spun him in the air. He giggled with delight.

"A baby! We're going to have a baby! A little pup to call our own," he shouted. If there was anyone in the house, they'd probably heard that, but it was fine. I wanted to shout it from the rooftops as well.

I set him down and gazed down at him. Tears streamed out of his eyes and I wiped them away with my thumbs.

"I wasn't even sure it was possible after—"

I shushed him. "That monster didn't deserve to have a baby with you. But we'll have one. And so close to Piers's baby's age. They won't be far apart. They'll be able to play and learn and grow together. Kenon will teach them all the tricks."

"You'll let Piers's baby stay part of the pack even though he's technically Shadowpine's." He wasn't asking. Not really. He just needed reassurance and I got that. The laws of old were strict on whose pack a pup was part of.

No ancient law was going to ever place that baby in harm's way. None.

My heart constricted. Even with all the progress we'd made, some doubts… not big ones, but some small doubts remained, and that was okay. It would take time. What was important was that my mate spoke them out loud instead of keeping them to himself. "Of course. There's no way I'd let them get their hands anywhere near him. That baby is not Shadowpine's, and never will be."

Niko shrugged. "Some packs would expel those pups to avoid the repercussions."

I rubbed my hands down Niko's arms. "Not this

pack. Piers's child will be one of us. He'll be Northbay, just like our baby is Northbay. Both of you are pack now. Not only that, but coming from the Alpha Omega line, those two pups will be like royalty. Blood will flow from anyone who attempts to treat them otherwise."

"How did we get so lucky?" Niko cupped my face in his hands and pressed a kiss to my lips.

I trailed my hand down his forearms. I always wanted to be touching him, caressing his skin. "Just fate, I guess," I said.

Chapter Twenty-Two

Niko

"They're getting so big," Dylan noted.

I leaned against Dylan as our pups played in the meadow, all five of them, three in their fur and two still yet to reach their first shift.

"Pretty soon they will all have their fur." He kissed the top of my head sweetly.

"Not all." I brought his hand to my middle. "Surprise?"

"Really?" he asked cautiously. "We're going to have another pup?"

A blood curdling scream and loud banging noise had us both up and running towards our pups…

Only it wasn't my blissfully beautiful dream turning into a nightmare—it was real life. The smell of smoke, the screams. Those were reality.

I sat up with a shot, Dylan already bounding out of

bed.

Screaming… rapid fire, like a machine gun… something else—maybe an explosion. It was all loud and chaotic.

"No! No! No! No! No!" This was my fault. I brought this here. Guns could only mean one thing—Carter and his crew were here and they weren't stopping at only getting us back—they were destroying the pack.

My pack.

"Stay here." It was an order. I'd never heard Dylan so Alpha than I did in that moment. More than anything I wanted to beg him not to go—plead with him to stay with me.

But our pack was in danger and he had to. This was who he was.

"Promise me." His eyes shone yellow. "My wolf won't let me go without a promise."

"I promise." I hated to. I wanted to find my brother and make sure he was okay, but while the screaming had ended, the noise from the weaponry carried on, which made the lack of screams somehow more terrifying.

"He doesn't follow shifter law." I climbed out of bed and cupped his cheek, my hands trembling. "You don't need to either."

"He will not breathe to see the sunrise." Dylan kissed me hard and ran down the stairs.

I followed him, locking the door behind him. Not in all my time here had he locked that door. Not once. But there I was doing so and knowing right well that it wouldn't be enough, but it would buy me time if I needed it. I locked the windows. Again, not something that would stop them, but the sound of broken glass would give me a few added seconds to get away or to fight.

I ran to the kitchen and found the largest knife I could. If they weren't going to play by shifter laws I sure as fuck wasn't.

The door knob twisted. Shit. I got distracted by the knives and hadn't gotten to lock the back door yet.

Maybe it was Darren. Dylan wouldn't leave me alone for long, he'd send someone here to the house.

It wasn't Darren. The scent of Carter slammed into me the second the door cracked open. Was it real? Or was I imagining things? I wished like hell that I was just dreaming, and that I'd wake in my alpha's arms. But it wasn't a dream.

"Little wolf, come out, come out." He was enjoying this. Fucker. He thought this was a game.

I'd show him a game.

I leapt over the counter, knife in hand, and managed to slice his arm as he came in through the now open door. It wasn't the direct hit to the heart I wanted, but it would slow him down.

He growled, more wolf than human. "You will regret that, you useless fucker."

I lunged again, this time grazing his side, the scent of his blood tickling my nose only an instant before he had my arm bent back with a snap.

I bellowed out in pain, hating to give him the pleasure of my pain, and make no mistake about it, he found great joy every time I so much as whimpered. At first I used to hide it, kept it all inside. It didn't take me long to discover that letting him get his satisfaction made the amount of torture significantly less because at the end of the day, Carter got what he wanted.

But not today. He would not get us—get our babies—and I would do anything within my power to save this pack. If only I had more power.

Never before had I wanted human weapons. That wasn't the way of things, but right now, I wanted one so badly I could taste it. I was no match for Carter teeth to teeth and claw to claw. Not even close and especially not with a broken arm.

His leg swept under me and I fell to the ground, my arm still in his hand. "Drop the knife or I will break both of them," he seethed. HIs eyes glowed a color I'd never seen before. He was wild with rage and out of control.

I wasn't sure I was even able to open my finger, not with my arm the way it was. I tried and failed, screaming out again, the exertion too much. "They don't work," I sobbed. "My fingers don't work."

He cackled as if that was the best thing he'd ever heard and used his other hand to slap the knife from me, the metal clinking on the ground the only way I knew I was successful. My fingers might as well not exist.

"Get up, vermin. We are taking a walk." He spit on me. "I said get up."

Somehow I managed to do so, the pain so severe I wasn't completely able to focus on what he was doing, which was bad—very bad. "This pack did nothing. Don't hurt them."

"The pack has what is mine. I came to get what is mine. If some of them get in the way and die, that's on them." He yanked me forward. "Let's get to your worthless brother."

We didn't defect. That would imply we were ever part of them. We weren't. We were property—toys. I knew better than to correct him. My only hope was that someone got them out of there and we would arrive at an empty house. I wouldn't live to see the day light if that happened, but my brother's baby and Kenon would. It was their only hope.

He dragged me straight there without a misstep. This was planned to a tee. What else did they know? Where were the rest of his crew and what had happened to Dylan?

"Get that useless slut of a brother," he seethed as he dropped me at the back door, kicking said door open. "You're his leader—call him or watch him die. I'll cut that pup right out of his belly and kill it too." He kicked me in the ribs. Another crack.

"You'll kill him and the baby anyway," I whispered, taking a breath in agony.

"No. They are mine to use as I see fit. Not that it matters to you. Look at your useless pile of flesh." He kicked me again. "Call. Him."

Cujo jumped out and pushed Carter to the ground. His growls ripped through the air. He'd caught Carter off guard since he didn't even know Cujo was here. His victory was short lived, though, the alpha flinging him across the porch. His head hit the post, his body lying there like a rag doll, the only sign of life his shallow breathing.

"Oh," Carter cackled with delight. "So the others are here. Good. More omegas for me to torture. Call. Them."

I tried. I did. But I couldn't do it. They needed to

run—to weaponize—to anything but give in. We were all going to die if they didn't.

The breeze shifted directions and I caught a whiff of Dylan's scent.

No. He couldn't be here. He would die. Everyone needed to flee. It was the only way.

"If you want to live, you will get out here now. My omegas and one worthless child were stolen from me. You don't have a lot of time left, maggot. Looks like I will need to find some new omegas to replace them here. There's some young ones around. You know how I like my omegas young." He stepped inside as he spoke and I dragged myself off the porch, dropping to the ground with a thud. Maybe—just maybe—he would follow me and the others could race out the front.

I called to my wolf.

He didn't answer.

I reached for him. If ever a time I needed him, this was it.

He was so far down, ignoring my calls.

"Run!" I cried out as loudly as I could, my lungs on fire.

The laughter that came from the porch would haunt me until my last breath. Never had I heard such evil, and I'd seen and experienced a lot. "It is going to be so fun watching you beg for your life." He cackled. "But not yet—not until this entire place is decimated and you watch."

Please! I begged my wolf and he came forward, taking my skin, my bones cracking in the most painful shift of my lifetime.

I rolled onto my feet, my right front leg completely lame. Three legs. I could cause some serious damage using only three legs. I had to.

I growled as I backed away from the house, trying to lure him to me. Dylan was close by. So close. Maybe—if I could just get him down, Dylan could help end him.

This wasn't an ordinary challenge. It was survival.

I growled again, this time making it known my beast was challenging him. Carter the man wouldn't care, but his animal was never far from the surface and he would.

One more growl and he jumped off the porch, shifting mid-air and ready to destroy me.

He never got the chance. Dylan's wolf met him mid-air. He had been closer than I realized.

I wasn't sure if I should help or back off, my helping only getting in the way. A whimper from the porch helped me decide. I bolted towards Cujo. If he was calling, he saw or sensed something I didn't.

It was only after I reached the porch and saw Kenon lying on Cujo that I saw why he'd really called to me.

I forced a shift, my arm bent to the wrong angle, and crawled over to them. "Kenon, you need to find Papa and tell him to run." The little boy shook his head, hugging Cujo close.

"Can you stand, Cujo?" He didn't move.

"Don't move," I ordered Kenon and went back to the porch.

I didn't think I had another shift in me, but I was ready if need be.

No one was getting near that child. No. One.

Guns shot off in the background, further away than earlier. Maybe not gunshots—maybe a bomb. Come to think of it, I hadn't heard or scented any other wolves. If the rest of Shadowpine were here, they weren't at the dorms with us.

Reaching the edge of the porch, I froze with terror like I'd never known before.

Blood—so much blood covered my mate, my stomach started to revolt. I couldn't lose him. I couldn't.

He and Carter circled each other, their teeth bared. Dylan's hair stood straight up on his shoulders. An open wound bled from his shoulder. Carter wasn't without injury. He limped heavily on his back leg and his face was mangled from a bite to his cheek.

Carter lunged toward Dylan, who leapt out of the way. He was almost in the clear, but Carter's jaws clamped on Dylan's back leg and pulled him to the ground. The thud reverberated through me and stole my breath. It was almost as if I was the one who'd been knocked down. Dylan yelped in pain and the sound tore at my gut like a knife. I couldn't stand by helplessly as my mate was hurt.

I dug around through the shreds of clothing left by Carter's shift and found his gun. I was no marksman. Not even close, but I'd seen him shoot enough to know the basics.

"Carter." I said his name with the same disdain with which he'd said mine so many times. "You probably shouldn't have let me watch you use this thing." I clicked the trigger with my good hand and pointed it in the sky, letting a shot fly so he would know I meant business. What I hadn't counted on was the force that pushed back on me, almost stumbling to the ground.

He jumped in my direction, as if forgetting Dylan was out for his blood. I fumbled with the gun. I'd meant to distract him, which I had. Mission accomplished. I just hadn't thought through the next part. He was now barreling towards where Kenon was holding vigil over Cujo.

Somehow I managed to get another shot out, the

gun pointed into the sky. I couldn't risk accidentally shooting Dylan or another pack member.

This time I did fall, Carter leaping into the air to attack, his body slammed to the ground by Dylan, his teeth around the other wolf's neck. Dylan didn't waste any time now that he had Carter down. His jaw closed around the other alpha's neck and he shook with more force than I'd ever seen him use. The tell-tale sign of a broken neck echoed in my ear before everything went silent.

Chapter Twenty-Three

Dylan

I tried to push myself to my feet. I barely got to my knees after shifting back to my human form. Carter, the alpha I had just killed, lay at my feet, unmoving, his blood still fresh in my mouth, and I wiped it away. It wasn't often that a wolf had to be put down. The only other time I'd had to deal with a wolf in this way was years ago when one of my Betas helped to kidnap the Greycoast Alpha Omega. I didn't take satisfaction in killing them back then, but I did this time. Carter deserved to die a thousand times over again. I only wish I could have done it sooner, before he'd gotten to my omega.

Killing Carter meant that I'd rid the world of an evil individual. It was the only choice that I had. And the world was a better place without him in it.

Niko rushed to my side and launched himself into my arms, knocking me back against the cold floor. I winced.

"I'm sorry," he said. "I'm so sorry." He touched me everywhere he could, his hands grazing over my limbs, mumbling his apology over and over again as if any of this were his fault. It wasn't. None of this was. The blame lay solely on Carter's dead corpse.

"Are you hurt?" I asked as I rubbed my hands slowly up and down his arms, checking his body over for injuries the same as he was doing to me. I still hurt, but my pain came second to his. He was my omega and nothing could stop me from making sure he was protected, safe, and cared for. Nothing.

Niko hissed in a breath when I touched his ribs. "They're fine," he lied. Nothing was fine about the sound he made at my mere touch.

"We need Reeva." I wasn't asking. "Now." Fine, I was bossing, but my wolf wouldn't allow it otherwise. "They can check you over. The baby—"

"Is fine," Niko said. He grabbed my hand and placed it over his abdomen. "Listen to your wolf. He will tell you the baby is fine."

I slowed my breathing and closed my eyes. Niko's heartbeat reached my ears and then another, more faint heartbeat joined the rhythm, faster than both of ours, but there.

"Our baby," I said.

Niko sighed. "Yes. He is strong."

"Like you." I rested my forehead against Niko's and breathed in his jasmine scent. I could have lost him today and that shook me to my core.

"Are you hurt, my alpha?" he asked.

"I'm fine," I said, though my shoulder ached, and I knew there was a gash on my back. It was possible my shin was broken where Carter had grabbed a hold of it. I was too afraid to look at it and even more afraid to try and stand on it. "Is everyone safe?" I asked.

Niko nodded. "I don't know. Cujo—Carter threw him and…" He got up and rushed to the porch. "Kenon!" he screamed.

I managed to get up and drag myself to him as he screamed again.

"Is here." Seymour came out holding the child. "He got away from me… I'm so careful but he got away from me." He let out a sob and the twins came up behind him, their hands settling on his shoulders.

"It was dark and he… he sensed something… there's no other reason he'd leave." Ralf reassured.

"Cujo—Carter hurt him." Niko's voice cracked. "Then Kenon… I was so scared."

I wrapped my arms around him from behind.

"You're going to be a powerful alpha one day, pup," I praised him. "You sensed one of your own was in trouble and went to help."

"Maybe next time leave it to the adults." Seymour held him even tighter. "Cujo."

I snapped my head back to his direction to find him walking this way. "Do you need a healer?"

He just trotted off into the house as if he hadn't understood a thing I'd said.

"We'll keep an eye on him," Seymour promised. "And Piers is fine, but he could probably use a hug from his brother when you are able."

"Tell him I'll be there once things are figured out," Niko said, his body now leaning against the rail.

Hutch came around the corner and shifted. "The premises have all been cleared, alpha. Carter was the only one here. He set up some human things to make it sound like we were surrounded, but the only scent is his."

Niko had explained the weaponry they had to me, the tool of deceit as well. Cowards. Wolves who used human weapons were nothing more than cowards.

It was a relief to hear that Carter had acted alone. I suspected as much by the time I got to the omega house, but the confirmation went a long way to soothe my beast.

Something in my gut told me that the rest of the

Shadowpine pack didn't want him here and hadn't any interest in finding the omegas. Maybe they were afraid of drawing the attention of humans or possibly just not wanting to miss out on the profit they'd give up by slowing down their drug trade. I had no idea, but when he showed up alone that day, it wasn't Carter the Pack Alpha, it was Carter the wolf. He just couldn't let Niko and Piers go and I suspected pride more than anything else.

"Sounds like something Carter would do," Niko said. "He probably wanted to save face by getting us back. Not to keep us—no, wolves that made him look bad had but one fate. He just wanted to prove he was Alpha."

"Not sad it didn't work out for him." Hutch growled, his eyes all wolf.

"Vaughn," I called out, scenting him near.

"Yes, alpha?" he answered as he jogged around from the other side of the dorms.

"Get this piece of trash out of my sight. Cut off his ear, so we can prove to Shadowpine that we killed him. Then burn the body," I said. I struggled to walk and Niko helped me, not that he was in much better shape than I. We needed Reeva. "I can't walk through the pack like this." Or walk through the pack at all.

"You can," Niko said. "I'll be at your side, helping

you. Let's take you to the infirmary. Let them see what you were able to overcome to keep us safe." So much pride filled his voice.

"No," I said. "Take me to the house. Reeva can come there. Then later we'll have a pack dinner."

"You need to rest," Niko argued. Stubborn omega.

"I need to show the pack that I'm fine." They'd all had a scare today. Many of the pack still remained in their houses, barricaded inside after that chaos when the artillery went off.

I gazed around for Darren and found him walking out of the omega dorms with Piers, Lewis, and Ralf at his side. Piers was looking for that hug, and if I thought I could stand up straight without Niko holding me, I'd have shooed him over there to do so.

"Darren, let the pack know it's safe to come out." That would give them some comfort.

"Who was shooting at the pack? I heard gunfire," Lewis asked. "If it was only Carter." Word sure got around fast.

"It was a decoy—like they set up with the humans," Niko called over my shoulder. "To get them away from us—from me. While the pack was scrambling to safety because of the explosions, Carter came after Piers and I."

"Always hiding behind human shit," Lewis scoffed.

"Let us know what the healer says," Piers called to us. "I need to know all three of you are safe."

All three of you. Me, my mate, and our babe. What more could an alpha ask for in life.

We started to take slow steps. With each one I gained more confidence that I wasn't going to face plant.

"Carter didn't anticipate that you'd fight him off as long as you did." I kissed Niko's head. "He didn't see how brave and strong you all were."

"I knew you'd come for me," Niko said, his arm running down to my lower back, the pressure of it being up with his broken rib getting to be too much. "I just had to be strong until then."

I kissed his cheek, trying to hide my wince in pain. He saw it though. I couldn't hide from my omega, just as he couldn't hide from me.

"You were very brave and strong and so quick on your feet. You saved Cujo, Kenon, your brother and the others… again."

I leaned against him as we walked toward our house, hating to make things harder for him, but needing to if I was going to arrive there. I knew it was stubborn to head there instead of the infirmary, but the wolves, especially the older ones, would need to see that. Their generation needed to visually see the strength of their alpha in times like these and if that meant I was stubborn? So be it.

Many pack members were out of their homes, looking around. The sun was barely coming up on the horizon, rays of light filtered through the trees. It was hot, even though it was only early morning. The smell of the gunpowder Carter had used lingered in the air.

"Was there any damage to any of the buildings?" I asked Ilyssa as I passed them. She seemed to be checking in with each of the pack members to ensure everything was fine.

She opened her mouth to answer me, but Niko ushered me along. "That can wait. Your Betas will come with a full report soon. You can worry about it then, first let's get you home."

I growled, but it had no malice in it. My mate only wanted to care for me. I didn't deserve him, but I was accepting the gift fate gave me regardless.

"Humor me, alpha." Such command in those three words.

I chuckled. "Fine. I can do that."

"After Reeva is done helping our sorry butts, I was hoping they could check on Piers and maybe bring him to the infirmary to be put on the monitor so we can make sure the baby is doing okay. That was a lot of stress tonight."

"First of all, there is nothing sorry about your butt. But yes, that's a smart idea about your brother," I said. "And you, my omega, how do you feel?"

Niko sighed and hugged me closer, which hurt yet was exactly what I needed at the same time. "Relieved. Is that bad?"

"No, not at all. I'm more relieved than ever to have him gone. With any luck, Shadowpine will leave us alone completely now." Based on what I knew about packs like that, the alphas were going to be too busy trying to gain power over the pack to be worried about us. Whereas my pack mourned the loss of each alpha as they met the goddess, packs like that saw it as an opportunity to move up.

"Perhaps," Niko said. He didn't sound as sure, and since he knew them better I figured it was best not to be too confident in my notion.

"If not, we'll be ready for them." There was no way I'd let them harm anyone in this pack if I had to bleed them all one by one. "We'll be more prepared next time."

"I know, alpha. I know you and our pack will do everything you can to keep us safe."

We reached the pack house and stood at the foot of the steps. I turned and faced my omega. I used my hand to brush the hair from his eyes. "Always, omega. I will always keep you safe."

He went up on his tiptoes and kissed me. His hands were on my hips holding me steady, while I balanced on one leg, trying hard not to put any weight on the one that I was sure was broken.

In a day or two it would heal, especially if I had the energy to shift back to my wolf form. But for now, rest would be necessary. Niko was right, I could wait to address my pack later. Them seeing me now, with my Alpha Omega at my side, would be enough to alleviate any of the concern they might have for my well-being.

News would spread like wildfire about what had happened that morning. Luckily, no one had had to witness the attack. Even more thankfully, no one appeared to be seriously hurt, my leg being the exception. The important thing was that the threat was taken care of.

"All right, you two, get a move on. I've got my handy dandy X-ray machine here. Let's get a look at that leg," Reeva said. They had managed to get an X-ray machine to my home. "Bet you're glad I convinced you to go military surplus, aren't you."

I chuckled. I was. At the time I thought it was to save on finances, but now I saw the added benefits. "I am indeed."

Niko helped me up the stairs and into the house.

"Did you happen to bring an ultrasound machine?" I asked, thinking perhaps we could see our baby on the screen.

Reeva shook their head. "Just the X-ray today. We'll focus on that baby of yours some other time. First we need him to have a healthy alpha and omega father. Niko, I'm afraid to mention it, because it appears that your wolf is managing all the pain for you, but your arm is definitely broken."

My eyes nearly bugged out of my head. I looked down at Niko's arm. It was twice its normal size and turning purple. "You told me you weren't hurt!" I wanted to kill Carter again, a thousand times over if necessary.

"Technically, I didn't answer when you asked," Niko said. "It doesn't hurt, I swear. It's the weirdest thing."

Reeva tsked. "It will. To bed, both of you. We'll get a look at those bones, get some tea into you, and we'll force a shift. That should fix the breaks. In a bit you can address the pack, to put their animals at ease. But for now, bed."

I wasn't going to argue. I grasped Niko's hand and the two of us went together. Right where we belonged.

Chapter Twenty-Four

Niko

"Ready?" Dylan came up behind me, his hands settling on my middle where our baby was growing.

I still wasn't showing to anyone who wasn't really looking hard and possibly using a microscope, but I felt our baby more and more each day.

It was still overwhelming to think about all that had happened in the months since I'd arrived at Northbay Pack, from my brother almost losing everything, to the night Carter took his last breath. I imagined it always would be, but I wouldn't change them for anything because each and every breath I took since we'd arrived led me to where I was right now. Even my stupid arm which had healed with a slight curve to it.

"Is it bad I just want to curl up in bed with you instead?" I tried to hold in a yawn and failed miserably.

"Reeva says it's normal." I gave him my best side eye in the mirror at his 'Reeva says' comment. Dylan had tons of them lately. He was all about making sure I had an idyllic pregnancy and it was both driving me bonkers and making me love him more.

Pregnancy sure messed with your emotions. At least mine did. That and being exhausted were my two big changes. Not that I complained. I was too ecstatic about having my babe growing inside of me to let any of that bother me.

Still, I didn't remember Piers being this exhausted and that did worry me a tiny bit. Not that he had time to let us see it… he'd gone from barely figuring out he was pregnant to needing to go on the run because his life depended on it. He was exhausted. We all were. I had so much respect for how long he held on like that, because getting downstairs to grab some toast in the morning had me ready for a nap now.

"Being cuddled up with you sounds almost as amazing as officially mating you in front of my pack." He winked at me in the reflection. "How about this… tomorrow you and I will spend the entire day in bed together?"

I turned in his arms to face him. "Something tells me that won't result in me resting." I nipped the mating mark I gave him.

"If you prefer to stay in bed alone—"

I nipped him a little harder. "No backsies." I smacked his ass playfully. "You and me in this bed all day long."

"Best. Mate. Ever." He punctuated each word with a kiss. "Ready?"

"Ready." I took his hand and we walked to the meeting place where our pack was already gathered, including his parents. I still didn't understand their hands-off approach to family, but I didn't need to. Dylan was fine with their out of sight nature. They doted on Ozzy's children, and I knew they would do the same with ours.

"I haven't even met them all yet," I whispered to Dylan as we entered the clearing. I'd gone out of my way to meet everyone or so I thought, but new eyes were in the field.

"That's because I invited some of the Greycoast Pack." He gave my hand a squeeze. "I wanted everyone I care about to see me formally mate the amazing omega Fate sent for me."

Someone in the crowd noticed us and a hush fell upon them. We worked our way up to where Gramps was standing and took our spots beside him.

Dylan turned his attention to the pack gathered before us; they awaited his words with bated breath.

"Northbay pack and friends, it is with great joy that I welcome you this evening to formally introduce you to my fated mate and your Alpha Omega. Niko is an omega of worth, and he brings strength, leadership, bravery, wisdom, and a future to our pack."

At first I thought he meant our baby, but then he turned to Seymour, Piers, Cujo, the twins, and Kenon.

"Tonight we welcome not only my mate, but five omegas and one tiny alpha, so brave and strong. They've always been Northbay. Ever since the day they bravely stepped foot on our territory they have been pack. Now we make it official. Piers, would you step forward."

Piers looked behind him to Darren, who still watched out for him like a hawk, even with Carter dead. Darren gave him a nod and Piers waddled over to where Dylan and I stood.

"Piers, I officially welcome you into the Northbay pack." Piers bared his neck to Dylan, who partially shifted his hand and sunk one claw into Piers's shoulder. It wasn't necessary to be marked by the Alpha to become pack in the truest sense, but we all met as a group and decided to stick with the ways of old to avoid any confusion if Shadowpine decided to try and claim ownership. Now we would scent like pack and have a visual marking of pack if it ever became necessary. I hated the reason for it, but to choose where you belonged was a powerful thing.

One by one, the pack members came up and bared their neck to my mate, and maybe it was the pregnancy hormones, but my eyes were leaking.

Piers went back to his spot and Dylan repeated the welcome with everyone, including Kenon, something Seymour insisted on. He didn't want there to be any doubt who his son belonged to. And then after the last neck was bared, it was our turn.

"Pack." Gramps sounded every bit Alpha with that one word. "It is a great privilege to perform our Alpha's mating ceremony. Fate has chosen well for him."

He held his hands out, indicating where the two of us would stand. "Tonight, as we accepted new pack in the way of old, we are going to witness the mating of our Alpha and Alpha Omega in the way of old."

He took out a leather twine. "Alpha Dylan, please take your mate's hand." He took my hand, his fingers wrapping around my wrist and mine wrapping around his. "The bond between mates runs deeper than we can ever truly understand." He wrapped the leather around us. "Tonight, with all of our pack as witnesses, we will bind you together physically as a symbol of this bond. But unlike this twine, the bond between you both can never be severed, not even by death."

The emotion was so raw in Gramps voice, my heart broke for him. To lose his mate. When I thought for that instant that I was going to lose Dylan… I couldn't have bore the pain the way Gramps had. His strength was far greater than my own.

He held our joined hands up. "Northbay pack and friends, prepare to run." Just like with the others, they came up one at a time and bore their neck, only unlike then, instead of going back to where they were, they went behind us and shucked their clothing. When the last one was done, my brother and the other omegas did the same, followed by the Greycoast Alpha and Betas. Never in my entire life had I felt so completely accepted… wanted… cherished.

Finally, Gramps came around and did the same. "Lead us on our run," he directed to me, and he joined the others behind us.

I answered with a single nod, afraid my words would fail me.

"Let's run." Dylan kissed me hard and fast… too fast. I wanted to luxuriate in his kiss, but that would have to wait. We had a pack to lead.

We walked around to where everyone was gathered, itching for their fur. "Let's run together, pack." I had practiced so many things to say when I heard I would start the run, but that said it all.

Dylan and I took three steps and shifted, our wolves taking our skin, shredding our clothes, the leather twine floating to the ground.

We didn't need it. Our bond was far greater than that leather. We'd overcome so much to be here and would continue to overcome every obstacle we came upon. We were fated, and as gramps had said earlier, nothing could break our bond.

The entire pack took off with a howl, running through the woods and tracing the perimeter of our land, as was tradition.

We circled back around and took our skin. "We forgot clothes," I teased as the other wolves put on the clothing they so carefully disposed of ahead of time.

"We have this." Dylan bent down and scooped up our binding. "Didn't even break… just like we won't break." Sure enough, it stood there perfectly connected.

"And never will." A warm cloth hit my back and I twisted around almost too quickly, having to catch myself from falling to see my brother there.

"Figured you'd want these." He still wasn't allowed to shift and had stayed behind with the few young that were skin bound. "You didn't tell me there was going to be food."

"Food?" I hadn't known about that part either, but inhaling, I scented at least three kinds of meat.

"Welcome to the Northbay Pack, where all parties include a pack meal." Dylan helped me on with my robe and then put his own on.

"If I had known that, I'd have signed up earlier," I sassed, leaning into him.

"I told you we need brochures, Alpha," Darren spoke from behind my brother.

"I didn't need a brochure to get you," Dylan teased right back.

"Welcome to the family." Ozzy joined us with his mate. "It's nice to see my brother so happy."

"Enough with sappy stuff," Reeva called over, "it's time to eat."

And eat we did. We ate. We laughed. We talked with all the pack members and our guests and then when we couldn't eat any more, we took our fur again and let our wolves play.

It was the perfect night even if the next day in bed was spent actually sleeping. We had time for the knotting fun—a lifetime of it.

Epilogue

Dylan

I threw a snowball toward the young pups who were all scrambling after me shouting "Alpha! Alpha! Over here!" I needed to get back to my home quickly, but I chose to spare a moment for the young pups.

I grinned at Kenon. He'd finally begun to come out of his shell. He played openly with the other pups as if he was born into our pack. I was happy to see that he would be a great role model for Piers's young pup, born just a few months ago, and my own pup who, if my wolf was correct, would be born today. On the night of the full Snow moon.

It was considered good luck for an Alpha's heir to be born on the night of a full moon and I couldn't wait for it to actually happen. My wolf had been restless for days; Niko's had as well. The baby had dropped and was now in position in the birth canal, according to Reeva. Niko had complained of back pain for the entire day.

Though I had been working in the pack, I had kept in close contact with him via texting with him, insisting he was fine, and for me to get back to work followed by various emojis that always had me cracking up. He'd adapted to all sorts of new technologies in the past couple of months.

He and the omegas even hosted regular movie nights at the dorms, which were attended by many of the other omegas and young wolves in the pack. Having the pseudo pack of omegas within the pack had proved to be pretty darn awesome.

Niko stepped into his role as Alpha Omega seamlessly. It was a role he was clearly born to have. He was a natural leader and an amazing partner. Ilyssa, the pups' teacher, called to the young pups and they took off toward the school house, running past the pavilion which was full of pack members enjoying their midday meals.

Later I'd come there for a pack meeting to announce the run for the night. Or perhaps I would have my own announcement. My wolf practically dragged me towards the house. My human feet were not moving fast enough for his comfort, even now that I was moving at a quick clip.

When I went inside, I found Niko in the living room, sitting on a large birthing ball Reeva had suggested we purchase. Though Niko had thought it was silly at the time, clearly it was doing something for him.

"How are you?" I asked and I kissed his cheek.

He took a deep breath and let it out through his nose. "I'm okay," he said through gritted teeth. "Just trying to breathe through these contractions."

I raised a brow. "Contractions? You're definitely timing contractions now?" That wasn't something he'd mentioned in his text unless he thought food emojis meant contractions.

"Yeah, they've been pretty steady." His voice was calm, but that didn't help me to keep my anxiety at bay. I was ready for this, right? I had to be. It was just all so… real. "Figured it probably wasn't something for a text."

I'd get back to that later. "Are you in any pain? I mean, you are but how much? What can I do?"

"No, I'm not in pain." he said. "Not much anyway. My wolf is managing it all still."

I took out my phone to call Reeva and he smirked, his body still bouncing up and down on the ball.

"I just called Reeva, though, before you arrived. They'll be here soon. Piers too." Of course he did. He had everything under control. The same couldn't be true for me. I felt helpless, and he hadn't even gotten to the whole birthing part of this having a baby thing.

"Good, good." The nerves were hitting me now; this was happening soon. It wouldn't be long before Niko's wolf couldn't hold back the pain, and he would feel it all suddenly. And then the baby would be here. It was a blessing that our wolves would take on that pain for us. But also, it made childbirth a bit of a guessing game. It was hard to tell when his wolf would relinquish and the birth could take place.

"Would you like to be in the bedroom?" I asked.

He shook his head. "I have everything ready here." He gestured to the floor where he had blankets laid, a table set up with water, and other things. Not boiling water, though. That was a thing, right? They always did that in movies.

"Clearly you've been busy today," I said.

Months ago we had attended Piers's birth. Niko and Piers had spent a lot of time researching the atmosphere they wanted to have while giving birth and from the looks of the room he hadn't changed one thing from that original plan.

Nothing about most of Piers's pregnancy had been within his control and watching the two of them plan away felt like an extra gift for him. Not that he once complained about anything. He was a sunshine and roses kind of guy and I admired that about him.

"Our pup will be born on the Snow moon." His hands went to his belly. "A good strong Alpha heir for you."

"Or omega," I said.

Niko grinned. "We both know this pup is an alpha. We have sensed it for some time now." We had, but if we were wrong, if he was a strong kick ass omega like his dad I'd be just as joy filled.

"I know, but I just want you to know that I would be happy with either one or both." Reeva seemed to think we wouldn't have trouble conceiving, their reasoning being, *Fate's got this.* But if we did, that would be fine too. Fate had already shined so beautifully upon us.

"Well, we aren't done yet, alpha." He flinched the tiniest of bits, then schooled his face. "We can have more."

"I'd like that," I said. "But let's get through this one first."

"Absolutely." He started bouncing again.

Reeva burst through the door and Piers followed after. In a flurry of activity, they had everything they needed set up and ready to get through it all. For all the *simplicity* Niko wanted for his birth, he also wanted human interventions *just in case.*

Niko bounced on his ball, breathing through the contractions that still remained mild, or at least he was acting like they were. His belly was tightening up something fierce, so fierce I could visually see it.

"This isn't fair at all," Piers said. "I was wailing by now."

"I'll feel it soon," Niko reassured him. "I'm sure of it. My wolf is getting tired."

I gripped his hand and squeezed, anxious to meet our pup.

His grip tightened until my hand was squeezed in a vise grip. Niko let out a mangled yell. By soon he had meant pretty much instantaneously.

"Good golly!" he cried. "Okay, I feel it now! That hurts, that hurts a lot."

"There. Now we're progressing," Reeva said. "You could stand if you'd like, or stay on the ball. But let's position you down a bit more and have your pants removed."

Everything happened so quickly. I did whatever Reeva told me to do, and held my omega as tight as I could. Piers had a washcloth, clearing the sweat from Niko's brow as the contractions intensified exponentially.

And then, with one very loud scream that echoed

through the entire territory, our baby boy was welcomed into the world.

Reeva quickly placed the squealing child in my arms. My wolf called out to him, welcoming him on to this plane, and he calmed. He blinked up at me with his beautiful eyes.

My breath caught in my throat and I blinked away tears. I wanted to see him clearly. "Oh my," I said. "This is my little boy."

"He is," Niko said.

"He's going to be strong like you," I said to Niko. "A proud Alpha leader for all." My throat closed as I choked back a sob.

"Good work, Niko," Reeva said. "You should heal up nicely. You managed to not tear at all, so your omega line will close on its own in a few hours. If you feel up to it later, I would be fine with you addressing the pack. It's not every day that we have an alpha heir born on the full moon."

"No, it's not," Niko said proudly.

I placed the baby in his arms. He was on the floor now, the birthing ball moved to the side.

"He's absolutely perfect," Niko said.

"He is," I agreed. "I love you, omega mine. How did I get so lucky?"

"I ask myself that every day." He looked up at me, tears in his eyes. "I love you, too, my alpha. We both do."

Claiming His Purpose

(https://amzn.to/3au LCuC)

Escaping his past, means embracing his Alpha.

Alpha Darren moved to Northbay after the death of his brother, looking for a new beginning—what he found was acceptance and a job as one of the pack Betas. After playing a pivotal role in protecting some pack members from a kidnapping, he is ready to just relax and enjoy his new pack. Too bad *fate* thought otherwise.

Omega Piers came to Northbay pregnant and barely alive. They took he and makeshift pack in, treating them like one of their own with an acceptance they never had known before. He could really learn to love it there. Too bad his *owner* thought otherwise.

When Piers and Darren met, they were immediately drawn to each other. Each a newcomer—each fleeing from their former lives in their own way. When Piers's past catches up to him, Darren does the only thing he can to save him—claiming him as his mate. It was a mating of necessity, nothing more. Both their wolves think otherwise. Spoiler alert: Their wolves are right.

Claiming His Purpose is a sweet with knotty heat M/M Mpreg Shifter Romance by the popular writing team of Jena Wade and Lorelei M. Hart. It features an alpha wolf still finding his way, an optimistic omega who is beginning to lose his sunshine, a mating of convenience, true fated love, and adorable babies. If you love your shifters hawt, your omegas strong, and your mpreg with heart, download your copy of Claiming His Purpose today.

Mpreg Titles by Jena Wade & Lorelei M. Hart

Greycoast Pack

Finding His Pack
Finding His Purpose
Finding His Potential
Finding His Passion
The Greycoast Pack: The Complete Collection
The Greycoast Pack: The Shorts

Northbay Pack

Claiming His Pack
Claiming His Purpose